Mail Order Mother
Book 28 in Brides of Beckham
Kirsten Osbourne

Chapter One

ANDREW DAWSON WALKED into his house at the end of a long day, thankful that Miss Pickering would have supper on the table when he got there. The young woman did everything she was supposed to do in a timely manner—mainly because she was afraid of her own shadow. She was the most ridiculously frightened woman he'd ever had the misfortune to have working for him, but she did her job, and that was all he needed from her.

When he walked into the kitchen, the sight before his eyes shouldn't have startled him, but it did. There was flour coating every surface, including the floor. *It must have been at least a twenty-five-pound bag.*

His angelic daughters were nowhere to be seen—not that he had angelic daughters. They were truly more demonic than anything else, but he didn't like to say that aloud. There was also no sign of Miss Pickering—and no sign of food.

"Is anyone here?" He was hungry, and after working for more than twelve hours, there should be food waiting for him.

Miss Pickering magically appeared from her quarters right off the kitchen. She was covered in flour from head to toe. Apparently, his daughters had "ghosted" her. Usually they did that when they were ready to get rid of a housekeeper, but he'd thought they were getting along well with Miss Pickering. "I would like to request a ride to the train station, Mr. Dawson. I can no longer work under these circumstances." It was the first time she'd met his eyes in the three weeks she'd worked there. Finally, she'd found her spine when she was ready to quit.

Andrew sighed. As soon as he'd seen the flour, he should have known, but somehow he'd been optimistic—ridiculously—that she would stay on. "Yes, of course. Do you have your things?" He wanted to suggest she take a bath first, but he'd done that with the first housekeeper—was that really only a year ago?—and she'd spit in his face.

"I've packed, but I'll collect them now." She stomped off into her bedroom, flour flying in every direction.

"Where are my girls?" he called after her.

"I've locked them in their rooms where they can't get into any more mischief."

Andrew sighed. He should let them out to clean up the mess, but . . . they'd want to go into town with him, and he wasn't about to reward their behavior. His sweet Marie had always been so much better at telling them no than he was. He'd let them out after Miss Pickering was gone. Hopefully he could find some canned goods at the mercantile while he was there. Miss Pickering hadn't ever been good with the girls, but the woman could cook. Now they would have to go back to beans.

She didn't speak on the entire drive into town, and he wasn't surprised. She'd already spoken to him more that day than ever before. The woman was simply not comfortable around men. At least that's what he'd surmised. She had never said anything about it.

As soon as he'd stopped the wagon, she jumped down and ran from him, her carpetbag in hand. She had lasted an entire three weeks, longer than any other housekeeper.

He went into the mercantile and nodded to the owner, Jonathan Snow. "I need to send a telegraph to the domestic agency."

Jonathan shook his head. "Sorry, Andrew. They said that there would be no more women sent out if this one left." The older man scratched his head, thinking. "The latest paper just came, and there's an ad for mail-order brides. If you were married to someone, she couldn't run off."

"Is there a way to telegraph this place?" Andrew knew they couldn't go long without help. His daughters would destroy everything.

Jonathan shrugged. "I'll try."

CAROLINE CASEY WALKED to Rock Creek Road to speak with Mrs. Elizabeth Tandy, a skip in her step. She went to church with Mrs. Tandy and had just discovered what the other woman did for a living—she was a real live mail-order bride matchmaker! Caroline had always longed for the romance of being a mail-order bride. Her parents thought she was crazy, but they hadn't denied her. They'd never denied her anything.

There had been many suitors there in Beckham for Caroline, but she'd rejected them all. None of them were the romantic figures of her dreams. No, she needed a real live hero who would sweep her off her feet and make her feel as if her insides were tingling. No more of the boring men in Massachusetts. There had to be exciting men out west somewhere, just dying for a woman to make their lives complete. She would *be* that woman!

She knocked on the door, which was answered by Mr. Tandy. "Hello, Miss Casey."

"Mr. Tandy! I was hoping to speak with your wife. I'm in need of her matchmaking services."

The blond man nodded once. "Yes, of course. Come in." He led her back to the last room on the left. "Elizabeth, Miss Caroline Casey is here to see you."

Elizabeth smiled. "It's good to see you, Caroline. Please, have a seat."

Caroline hurried to the sofa and sat down. She'd never been in the Tandy home before, but it was bigger and more beautiful than she'd dreamed. "I want to be a mail-order bride!"

"I had a feeling you'd come see me." Elizabeth leaned forward as much as she could around the baby she was carrying. "Why do you want to be a mail-order bride? There's hard work at the other end of this journey."

"Oh, that's fine. I *like* to do hard work." Caroline didn't spend five days a week volunteering at an orphanage because she was lazy. "I like the romance of it all."

Elizabeth frowned. "I'm not sure you're going to find romance as a mail-order bride. Most of these men are looking for someone who is willing to help them build up a farm or a ranch. Someone who will take care of their children."

"I can do those things! I promise you, Elizabeth. This is what I want!"

"All right. Let me think about who is right for you." Elizabeth sat in concentration for a moment. "I got a telegraph from a man desperate for a bride just yesterday. Let me pull it out. Bernard was able to investigate him by telegraph, and he has an impeccable reputation, though his daughters are known to be troublemakers." She went through a batch of papers and handed one to Caroline.

Caroline read through the telegram. "Texas? I've never been to Texas!" She got more excited by the moment. "Yes, I want to marry him. When can I leave?"

Elizabeth laughed. "I can send a telegraph back. I usually do things by letter, but it seems like the two of you are in a huge hurry for everything."

"I know I am. I'm ready to start my adventure!"

"I hope you know what you're getting into." Elizabeth frowned at Caroline for a moment. "You have loving parents. You have a good life here. Why do you want to do this so badly? I'm a little worried about you."

"I need a change. Something *different*."

"This will definitely be something different." Elizabeth smiled as her husband brought in a tray of cookies and tea. She poured two cups. "Thank you, Bernard."

When they'd finished with their tea, Elizabeth smiled. "I'll send a telegraph first thing, and I'll send a note over to your house with the response. Will that work?"

"I'll be at the orphanage all day," Caroline said, getting to her feet. She would have children. A new husband. Picnics by streams and reading poetry by a fire. Life was finally going her way.

THREE DAYS LATER, CAROLINE sat waiting for her train, Elizabeth at her side. "I'm so excited. In just a little over a week, I'll be married!"

"I just want you to remember that no matter what happens, you're welcome to come home. If he hurts you in any way, I will personally pay for your train ticket." Elizabeth shook her head at Caroline. "Are you even listening to me?"

"Of course I am. I'm just so excited it's hard to concentrate!" Caroline wanted to break into song and dance like she'd once seen in a musical when she went with her stepmother to New York City. She wasn't certain how Elizabeth would react to her antics, though, so she stayed put.

"You're going to be on the train for a very long time. I hope you brought something to keep you occupied." Elizabeth smiled at her.

"Oh, of course. I brought books and some sewing. I'm making myself a new apron. And I'm hemming the dress I made for my wedding. And I brought my crochet hook and some thread. I think I might make a collar for a dress." Caroline was excited for the long, boring hours on the train. She didn't tell Elizabeth, but she was thinking about writing some poems for her new husband. She would read them to him on their wedding night. She sighed happily.

When the conductor called for everyone to get on the train, Caroline hugged Elizabeth. "Thank you for making this possible!"

"I hope this marriage is everything you dream of."

"Oh, I know it will be! I'm just certain of it."

Caroline picked up her carpetbag, knowing that her much-bigger trunk was already loaded onto the train. Her new life was going to begin in just a few days.

ANDREW STOOD ON THE train platform, wearing his Sunday best. He wanted to make a good impression on his new bride. He knew little about her other than the fact that she considered herself an excellent cook, and she said she was good with children. It would have to do.

His girls stood at his sides, both of them dressed in their newest dresses, which he realized were not nearly long enough for their rapid growth. At twelve and ten, his girls were becoming ladies, and they really did need a mother's touch. His sweet Marie had died a year before, and he'd been struggling with them ever since.

When the train pulled into the station, he told the girls to straighten up and smile. His older daughter, Victoria, pulled her face into a grotesque version of a smile, while Amy merely grimaced. Neither of them was looking forward to having a new mother, but he didn't care. This was the answer.

Five people got off the train there in Whistle Stop, Texas. The town had been formed when the railroad came through, and it was very small and simple. Everyone knew everyone, and there were few businesses.

First a couple stepped off, and Andrew waved to them. He knew the Rileys had taken a trip back east to visit her aging parents. Then a young man he didn't recognize got off the train. He was probably there to work at one of the local ranches. He looked like a youngster from back east who wanted to be a cowboy. Following him was a tall woman who looked as if she'd just eaten an entire jar of pickles, her face was so sour. He felt a moment of panic that the woman could be his bride, but she walked over to a farmer in town and embraced him.

He waited for another full minute before a woman stepped off the train. She looked to be in her early twenties, which would fit the description Caroline had given of herself. She looked straight at him with a smile and hurried in his direction. "You must be Andrew Dawson. It's so good to meet you. I'm Caroline Casey, and I'm going to be your beloved wife."

Beloved? Andrew nodded. "I'm Andrew, and these are my daughters, Victoria and Amy."

Caroline's face lit up as she looked at the girls. "I'm so excited to meet you. I'm going to be the best wife and mother I know how to be. I promise you this!"

He thought for a moment about telling her that he was really just looking for a housekeeper, but he didn't know how to say it in a way that wouldn't upset the girl. She seemed very excited to be there. "The preacher is waiting to marry us in his home. It's just a block from here. Would you mind walking?"

"Oh, not at all. I hope there's a place for me to change into the dress I made for our wedding. I finished hemming it on the train." Caroline smiled at him sweetly. "My trunk is on the platform."

"Trunk?" He'd been expecting her to arrive with just a carpetbag like all of the housekeepers. "I'll get it in the wagon."

"What do you do for a living, Andrew? Is it all right if I call you Andrew?"

He blinked a few times, wondering what he'd gotten himself into. Was it too late to back out? "Yes, of course."

"And what do you do for a living?" She smiled beguilingly at him.

"I'm a rancher."

"Oh, cows! I love cows!" She pointed to her trunk, and he found himself obeying her pointing finger, walking toward the luggage so he could load it.

As soon as he headed away, Caroline turned to the girls. "Now, you're Victoria, right? How old are you, Victoria?"

"I'm twelve, and I don't need a mother, a housekeeper, or a nanny. I can take care of myself."

Caroline smiled. "Of course you can! I'm so glad that you're capable. That means you can help me settle in. I know nothing about being a rancher's wife." Then she looked at the younger girl. "Amy, right? How old are you?"

"Ten." Amy said nothing else and instead stood glaring at Caroline.

"You're practically a lady!" Caroline saw that her trunk was back, and she watched as Andrew loaded it for her. "I wasn't able to bring friends along to stand up with me, so I was hoping the two of you would be my bridesmaids. Do you mind?"

Victoria looked at Amy before shaking her head. "I don't mind."

Amy seemed confused for a moment. "I'll do it."

"Oh, good. I hope there's a place for us to pick flowers on the way. Don't you think we should all have flowers to hold?"

"We should be able to find some bluebonnets," Victoria said, still seeming very surprised. "Do you like bluebonnets?"

"Would you believe I've never even seen a bluebonnet? You'll have to show me what they look like." Caroline linked arms with the girls, leaving Andrew to follow in their wake.

Andrew frowned. "The preacher's expecting us soon. We don't have time to wander around looking for flowers."

"Of course, we do, Andrew. A woman only gets married once, and she needs to have flowers. Wouldn't you agree, girls?"

"I guess . . ." Victoria said.

"See? The girls agree with me, and you're outvoted, Andrew." Caroline kept the girls' arms firmly in her grasp, knowing they would both rather run away than deal with their crazy future stepmother. She didn't care, though. She already loved them with everything inside her. They were her daughters, after all.

Finally, one of the girls pointed to a field. "Bluebonnets," Amy said softly.

"Oh, we must pick a bouquet for each of us. Bluebonnets are beautiful!" It was a little hard for Caroline to believe just how many flowers were in bloom. When she'd left Massachusetts, there was still snow on the ground. She released their arms, and all three of them began picking the pretty flowers.

Andrew stood watching the scene before him, more than a little shocked. How had she gotten the girls to do something she wanted? And how long would it be before she was covered in flour and demanding a ride to the train station?

When they'd all picked the flowers they wanted, Caroline returned to him. "Well, we have enough flowers, I think. Now let's get married." Her smile kept stunning him. Why was she so happy?

He cleared his throat. "Preacher's house is this way." Andrew had always been a rather quiet man, doing what he needed to do to keep his ranch going and his wife happy. Now here this woman was, and she . . . well, she was something outside of his realm of understanding. No one was that happy.

Truly, he'd expected a mail-order bride to be rather homely, but Caroline was pretty. Her blue eyes seemed to sparkle at him.

The four of them walked toward the small parsonage attached to the church. When Mrs. Nelson, the pastor's wife, opened the door, Caroline smiled happily. "We're here for our wedding! Is it all right if I change first? I just finished sewing my wedding dress on the train, and I would be devastated if I couldn't wear it."

Mrs. Nelson blinked a couple of times before opening the door wide. "I'll show you to a room where you may change."

"Thank you so much. I really appreciate your hospitality." With those words, Caroline disappeared around the corner with Mrs. Nelson.

Andrew stared after her for a moment, before looking down at his girls, who still had flowers in their arms. "She's different."

Victoria nodded. "Very."

"I'm not sure how she's going to fit in," Amy said, still staring at the spot where Caroline had disappeared as if she was waiting for her to magically reappear.

The three of them stood in uncomfortable silence as they waited for Caroline to come back. He realized as he stood there that Marie had been the glue holding their family together. She'd been the one who kept conversations going and made them all happy. Since her untimely death, they'd all stood around, not even really speaking to one another. Maybe Caroline was what they all needed. He certainly hoped so, because she was who they had.

When she returned, she made a grand entrance, spinning around as soon as she was in sight, making her skirts swirl around her. "What do you think? I made it myself!"

"It's very nice," Andrew said after waiting for a moment for one of the girls to say something. Neither did. They just stood watching her as if waiting for her to do something absolutely crazy and fly away.

"Thank you. Now let's get married, shall we?"

Andrew couldn't help but wonder what she expected of the marriage. She seemed like any bride would on a wedding day. Very excited. Of course, the nervousness was missing. Who wasn't nervous when they married a stranger?

When Pastor Nelson pronounced them man and wife, Caroline turned her lips up to Andrew expectantly. He went to kiss her cheek, but she turned her head so her lips met his and wrapped her arms around him, kissing him with a great deal more passion than was proper at a wedding ceremony.

The pastor coughed to break up the kiss, and Andrew stood staring down at the creature who had gotten off the train, wondering what on earth he'd gotten himself into.

Chapter Two

IN THE WAGON ON THE way to the ranch, Caroline kept up a steady stream of conversation, seeming not to notice that she was the only person talking. It was only when she mentioned school that one of the girls responded.

"I bet the two of you are ready for summer vacation from school. We'll have a wonderful time this summer. I can't wait to have you to myself all day long!" Caroline said.

"There isn't a school here," Victoria said.

"There's no school?" Caroline was shocked. She thought there were schools all throughout the country. "But how do you learn?"

Amy shrugged. "Mom taught us until she died, but she wasn't very fond of learning."

"Well, then we have a lot to make up for, don't we? I even have some things I've written myself. I brought my old schoolbooks, thinking they might be needed. Oh, we're going to have a wonderful time learning all there is to learn!"

Andrew looked at her out of the corner of his eye. "The girls aren't going to be doctors or lawyers."

"Why not? They certainly seem bright enough! But I'll teach them things that will help out around the house, too, so they can make their own decisions. I'll teach them to cook and sew and clean . . ."

Victoria groaned. "We *already* know how to clean."

Caroline turned around to look at the girl who was perched atop her trunk in the back of the wagon. "That's wonderful!"

Amy frowned at her. "Why is it wonderful?"

"Because then we can do that together and sing while we work."

"Sing?" Victoria asked.

"Certainly! Haven't you learned that singing while you do anything makes the time fly by? I just love to sing. And I'll teach you to dance with the broom!"

"Are you good at it?" Andrew asked. He wasn't the best singer himself, but he didn't want to spend the rest of his days listening to a woman who couldn't carry a tune in a bucket. And she'd be gone by the end of summer anyway.

"No one has complained yet!" Caroline told him. "Oh, the meadows are practically alive with bluebonnets. No wonder you girls suggested those for our bridal bouquets. When we get to the house, we'll press the flowers so we can keep them forever." She hugged her bouquet to her, not realizing she'd lost her audience. Even if she had, she probably wouldn't have cared. This was the happiest day of her life.

It took more than thirty minutes to get to the ranch, and she was surprised at the sheer size of it. "Oh, what a beautiful house. And just think, I get to be the person to clean it every day." She was overjoyed at the prospect of keeping it clean for her new family. "How many more children do you want?" she asked Andrew. "I want at least a dozen, so we'll need ten more, since you've already given me the gift of two daughters."

Andrew hadn't even thought about having more children. How could he when the ones he had were hellions? He didn't answer, and she didn't even seem to notice as she flitted onto the next subject.

While he unhitched the horses, the girls took her inside and showed her around. The kitchen seemed to be piled high with dishes, and there was a white residue all over. "Is that flour?" she asked.

The girls exchanged a look and nodded. "I tried to make a cake after the last housekeeper ran away, but I couldn't make it work. I made a bit of a mess," Victoria said.

"We tried to clean it," Amy said.

"We'll all do it together!" Caroline said with enthusiasm. "I can't wait! I think we'll start our day with some cleaning before we get down to schoolwork."

"You mean on Monday?" Victoria asked. "Because today is Friday. Dad will go back out to work for the rest of the day, and you'll need to make supper."

"We'll all make supper together." Caroline clapped her hands as if she'd just come up with the best idea she'd ever had. "Let's go look around now. Show me where I'll sleep, and then show me your rooms. Oh, I just want to see everything."

Victoria opened a door off the kitchen. "All of the housekeepers slept here, so that's probably where Dad will want you."

Caroline frowned. "Why would he want me here? No, this will be the guest room. I'll give it a good cleaning the first chance I get. I can see there's going to be plenty to keep me busy here. Just the way I like it." She was the new wife and mother. Why would she be banished to the housekeeper's room? She knew it would never be that way.

Amy looked at Caroline as if she'd lost her mind before leading her up the stairs. "The family sleeps up here." She opened a door at the top of the stairs. "This is Dad's room."

Caroline set her carpetbag down just inside the door. "This room will be perfect for me, then. I'll wait until later to unpack." She could tell the housekeeper had been gone for a short while. Things were messy but not dirty—well, other than the flour covering the entire kitchen. She'd have the whole house in shape in no time.

The room next to theirs was a nursery. There was a crib and a yellow quilt hanging over the rail. "What a pretty little room."

"It was for the baby," Victoria said softly, looking at the room as if she'd never been in there.

"Baby?"

"Mom died in childbirth, and the baby, too. It was a boy." Amy walked out of the room and to the next, as if she hadn't just given away a great deal of information. "This is my room."

The bed was made neatly, and the room looked perfect. "Did you clean it before I came?"

Amy shook her head. "No, my room always looks this way."

Next, they went to Victoria's room, and it was exactly the opposite of her sister's. The bed was unmade, and there were clothes all over the floor. "Let's make your bed together, Victoria," Caroline suggested.

"You can do it, but I don't feel like it." Victoria leaned against the wall with her arms folded, as if waiting to see what Caroline would do.

"You're giving me the joy of serving you? Why thank you, Victoria." Caroline hurried over and made the bed, plumping the pillows and leaving it as neat and tidy as she herself would have liked. She could already tell she was going to have to come up with some kind of strategy for getting along with her cranky new stepdaughters, but she had no idea what it would be.

When she'd finished, she smiled. "What haven't I seen yet?"

"The parlor," Amy said, looking back and forth between her sister and her stepmother. She obviously wanted to get along with both and wasn't sure how to make that happen.

"Let's see the parlor, then. And then I'm going to start supper. If you girls would like to help me with supper and cleaning the kitchen, that would be wonderful."

"I'll help." Amy looked at her sister to see what she'd say.

"I'll watch." Victoria had a look on her face that told Caroline she thought she'd won.

"Let's go." Caroline linked her arm with Amy's, and the two of them led the way down the stairs to the parlor. "Oh, this is a wonderful room for being together as a family. I can't wait to teach you girls to sew in here."

Back in the kitchen a few minutes later, Caroline looked in the ice box for food. She found some chicken. "Is there more flour that didn't end up on the floor?" she asked Amy.

Amy nodded. "In the pantry."

"There's a pantry?" Caroline thought she was in heaven. This house was a cook's dream. Not many people she knew had pantries.

"Mom insisted that we have one when we moved in. She said it was impossible for her to be climbing up and down cellar stairs in her condition."

"So you moved here while your mother was carrying your brother?"

Victoria responded to the question from the table, where she sat watching. "You don't need to be asking questions about our mother. You're *never* going to take her place."

"I'm not trying to. I was just hoping you could find a *new* place for me." Caroline said nothing else as she disappeared into the pantry and found flour. She gathered up the other things she needed and hurried back into the kitchen. "Do you girls like chicken and dumplings?"

"It's my favorite," Amy said. "Victoria's, too!"

"Mine, too. We'll have a good hearty meal of chicken and dumplings for supper tonight." Caroline put the chicken on to boil, thrilled that there was a water pump right there in the house. This place really did have all of the modern conveniences. Why, there was even a water closet!

While the chicken boiled, she got out the broom and worked on getting the flour off the floor. She could tell the girls had made a small effort to clean it, but their hearts hadn't been in it. While she cooked, she sang softly, a tune about a sailor who was lost at sea. It wasn't a happy song, but it was pleasant enough. She had learned it from her father, who had been a ship's captain her entire life.

While she swept, stopping at times to scrub up the flour that had been ground into the wood, Amy filled a bucket with soapy water, and she scrubbed the places that were already swept. The two of them worked together perfectly, while Victoria glared at both of them.

When she'd finished the floor, Caroline sat down at the table. "That was fun."

Victoria frowned at her. "Why was it fun?"

"Because I chose to make it fun. Now I'm going to roll out dumplings. Would you like to help cut them? Or are Amy and I going to have all the fun again?"

"I'll watch."

"Suit yourself!"

Caroline poured a bit of flour onto her work table to get it ready for the dough she would be slapping onto it, and she mixed the dough, while Amy finished scrubbing the floor. Then the girl washed her hands, and the two of them rolled out the dough for the dumplings and cut it. While they did, they sang Three Blind Mice as a round, going faster and faster as they went. Both of them were laughing before they were finished.

Together they dropped pieces of dough into the broth they'd made and watched as each piece rose to the top. "I've never helped make dumplings before, but it really is fun," Amy said. "I like that you make ordinary chores seem like fun."

From behind them, Caroline heard the front door slam. She didn't have to turn around to see that Victoria had left the two of them alone. "Victoria doesn't like me," Caroline said.

"She misses Mom. She's refused to do any household chores since she died, because Mom never made us help. I think seeing someone else cleaning the house makes her miss Mom even more." Amy looked sad as she talked about their mother.

"I'm sure she was a wonderful woman, and I'm sorry you lost her so young. I know when my mother died, I never thought I'd be able to like my new stepmother. I was thirteen, and it seemed like she was trying to be my mother. But I knew she wasn't." Caroline shook her head. "It didn't take me long before I realized that having her in my life was better than having no woman to look up to at all, and we became friends. I decided then that people need to be given chances before we judge them."

Amy smiled. "We scared off all the housekeepers," she confided. "That's why Miss Pickering left. We ghosted her."

"You ghosted her? I'm not sure what that means."

"We set up a bag of flour above her doorframe, and when she opened the door, the flour poured onto her head. And then she was all white, like a ghost."

Caroline laughed. "I'll be sure to be ready to be ghosted, then."

"I don't want to play tricks on you. I'm sure Victoria will, though." Amy shrugged. "It's her way of saying no one can be her mother."

"Thanks for the warning." Caroline dropped the last of the dough into the broth and washed her hands. "What time does your father come in for supper?"

"When it's dark."

"Even in the summer when it stays light out longer?"

Amy nodded. "Always."

"Then I'll be sure to pack him extra food in the summer so he won't be hungry all day." Caroline glanced out the window and noticed the sun was already setting. She set the table. "Will Victoria find her way back in?"

"She always comes back when she's hungry."

"She sounds very smart." Caroline finished everything, putting some of the flowers from her bouquet in a vase at the center of the table.

"That looks really nice. No one has cared about making the table look nice since Mom died."

Caroline could almost feel the ghost of the dead woman there in the room with them, because her presence was clearly still there. "You miss her a lot, don't you?"

"Not as much as Victoria does. Victoria still cries herself to sleep almost every night."

"She sounds like she was an amazing woman. I wish I could have met her and been her friend." Caroline went to the stove and stirred the dumplings, for a moment wondering if she'd done the right thing. But then she remembered who she was, and she straightened her shoulders. It was almost completely dark.

The door opened then, and Andrew came in with Victoria close behind him. "Are you hungry?" Caroline asked, her normal enthusiasm back in her voice. "Amy and I cleaned the kitchen and made chicken and dumplings."

Andrew looked at Victoria. "You didn't help?"

"Watching them made me miss Mom."

Caroline had felt bad for the girl until that moment. She was playing games with her father's emotions, and it was obvious to her if not to her father. "She watched and kept us company," Caroline said with a smile, wondering what it was going to take to get through to the girl. "Sit down while I serve."

Andrew washed his hands before sitting down at the head of the table. He waited until everyone was sitting before bowing his head and saying a brief prayer. "This looks delicious." He still felt uncomfortable with the woman, but he wasn't going to let her efforts go without praise.

"I hope it tastes as good as it looks." Caroline took a bite, and she realized it was the best batch of chicken and dumplings she'd ever made. She was thrilled they'd come out so well on her first day with her new family.

Amy took and bite and smiled. "They're better than Mom's!"

Victoria's face crumpled at her sister's words. "They are not! They're not nearly as good as Mom's." With that the girl jumped up from the table and ran to her room.

Andrew stood up to follow her, but Caroline shook her head. "I think she needs a little time alone. I was a little older than Victoria when I lost my mother. She just needs some time."

He looked at her for a moment. "Don't let her disrespect you."

"Oh, don't worry. I can stand up for myself." She finished eating and put her bowl into the basin. "Is anyone else finished?" After refilling Andrew's bowl, she cleared away Victoria and Amy's dishes. "Would you like to help with the dishes tonight?"

Amy nodded. "I really do like to help."

"I'm glad." Caroline started to hug the girl, but realized she may need a little more time. "Do you like to wash or wipe?"

"I like to wash, if you don't mind. I always have to wipe because I'm the youngest."

"Then tonight, you get to wash."

Andrew plowed through two more bowls of the meal while watching his new wife with his younger daughter. Amy was warming up to Caroline and not taking her sister's side about everything as she'd done with the housekeepers. Maybe she'd be good for them, despite first impressions.

Caroline took his bowl. "Do you want more?"

He shook his head. "No, thank you. I appreciate you cooking as soon as you got here. I'm sure you're exhausted." Now that he was actually looking at her, he could see dark circles under her eyes. "It must be hard to sleep on a train."

She smiled. "It wasn't easy, but I got a little sleep." She hurried to Amy with the bowl. "Tomorrow night, I'll make sure to take the time to make dessert." As soon as the words were out of her mouth, a thought formulated in Caroline's head. Maybe dessert would be the answer to Victoria's nonsense. She could only hope.

After the dishes were finished, Amy dried her hands. "I'm going to go see if Victoria is all right."

Caroline nodded. "That sounds good. Make sure she knows that she's welcome to have more to eat whenever she's ready."

Andrew watched Caroline, wondering what she had up her sleeve. She was obviously plotting something, and he hoped it was for the good of his family. He had a feeling she would be able to destroy just as she could build up.

Caroline smiled at him. "So what time do you like to eat in the mornings?"

"I prefer to be out of the house and working by sun up, so five thirty or six would be preferred."

"Do you have hired hands to help you?"

"I couldn't run a ranch this big without help." He shrugged. "I'd hoped for boys to help me run things, but so far, I have two girls."

She grinned at him. "I'll do my best to give you sons."

He was stunned for a moment. "Oh, I didn't mean . . ."

"I did."

Chapter Three

AFTER THE GIRLS WERE in bed, Caroline retrieved one of the poems she'd written for Andrew on the train. Her handwriting was shaky and a little hard to read, but she endeavored to read it to him. She needed him to know that she was his devoted wife forever.

I've never seen your face.
But I know that I will love you.
I'm ready to meet you now.
As soon as the train comes through.
Poems are harder than I thought.
But writing them is good for me.
I will be there in a mere three days.
My love burns for thee.

After she'd read it to him, she smiled proudly. She'd never written a poem, but she'd been inspired by him to do so. Perhaps someday, she'd be a famous poet like Longfellow or Emerson.

Andrew stared at her in shock, wondering why anyone would write something so horrific for a total stranger. The woman was clearly lacking in sanity. Was she right for his children? "Thank you," he said, because she clearly expected him to say *something*.

"You're welcome." They were in the parlor, and she hurried over to sit close to him on the sofa. "Amy thought you'd want me to stay in the housekeeper's room off the kitchen, but I knew better, so my things are in your room."

He looked at her for a moment. "You wouldn't like some time to get to know one another better before we share the marital bed?"

"Why would I?" she asked. No, she was looking forward to sleeping in his bed. The kiss they'd shared at the church had caused her heart to beat faster and *things* to happen inside her.

He frowned. "I knew my wife for almost a year before we married. I thought most women would prefer to know the man they were . . . consummating their marriage with." He wanted the time, but how could he tell her that? She seemed particularly dense about her place in his home.

"Not me. Do you want to give me five minutes to change?"

He nodded, but as she was hurrying out of the room, he called her back. "Wait, Caroline."

She turned to him. "Yes?"

"I'm not ready for a physical relationship. I buried my wife just a little over a year ago, and I expected to spend the rest of my life with her. I need time."

"Oh. So we'll just lie in bed together without touching? Is that what you want?"

He shook his head. "For now, I think it would be best if you stayed in the housekeeper's room off the kitchen."

"I see." Caroline had never felt so rejected in her entire life. Not even when Victoria had made it clear she wanted nothing to do with her earlier. "How long do you think this situation will last?"

"I have no idea. Until we've gotten to know one another better."

She frowned. "Then you'll be writing me love poems?"

He shook his head, his eyes wide with what looked like panic. "I could never!"

"But you'll find some way to woo me? Perhaps a picnic after church? Or reading love poems to me by a fire?"

"There are other ways for us to court."

"Why am I expected to court my husband? That part is over, and we skipped it. That's what a mail-order marriage is all about. Not having to do the courting and the wooing. We skip straight into going to bed together."

He closed his eyes. He'd never expected to be pressured for sex by his new wife. "I . . . I don't feel comfortable with that. I'll find a satisfactory way to woo you. I promise."

She put her hands on her hips, as enthusiastic about this conversation as she was about any other. "If you reject me now, you're going to have to do a good job of wooing me to get me into your bed. You have ten minutes to change your mind while I clean the room off the kitchen. Make sure you're making the right decision for all of us."

Andrew sat on the sofa and stared at the spot she'd vacated when she flounced off to clean the housekeeper's room. The woman was . . . something else was the only phrase that came to mind.

He didn't see how the girls would be affected if they slept together or not, so he didn't consider them. No, what he needed to think about was how comfortable he would be sleeping with her without touching her. She was a young beautiful woman, and it had been more than a year since he'd had relations. But he would feel as if he was betraying Marie's memory if he agreed to sleep with her.

He sighed. There was no right decision. Caroline obviously was feeling rejected by him, but having a real marriage with her seemed completely out of the realm of possibilities.

She walked back into the room while he was still arguing with himself. Standing in front of him, she frowned. "Have you made up your mind yet?"

"I—I'm not ready to sleep in the same bed as you."

"Fine. But you'd better be getting your knees toughened up then, mister."

"Why should I toughen my knees?"

"Because you'll be on them begging before I am ever in your bed." With those words, she went into the little bedroom on the first floor and closed the door behind her. She put her clothes in the drawers and even set the photograph of her with her father and stepmother on the bureau. It would be a cold day in Texas before she'd give him the satisfaction of sharing his bed.

She threw herself down on her bed and reached for her favorite book. She would read *Jane Eyre* while he spent the night in his lonely bed.

NO MATTER HOW TIRED she was, Caroline was up before dawn the following morning, cooking breakfast for her new family. She had noticed some syrup in the pantry, so she made pancakes and bacon.

When Andrew walked into the kitchen a short while later, he walked over to Caroline and wrapped his arms around her from behind. He'd had a hard time sleeping, knowing that his beautiful new wife was sleeping under the same roof he was . . . apart from him. He wanted to change his decision of the night before.

Burying his face in her neck, he apologized. "I'm so sorry for making you sleep downstairs last night. I've changed my mind. Will you move your things to my room today while I work?"

Caroline laughed. "No, I will *not*. You had your chance to change your mind, and you didn't. Now you will woo me, or you will sleep alone for the rest of your days."

He was shocked at her refusal. "But . . ."

"There are no buts. I told you to change your mind or woo me. Period. You didn't change your mind, so now you will spend your days trying to think of ways to get me into bed with you." She flipped his pancakes onto his plate and added bacon. "Breakfast is ready. I didn't see a coffee pot, or I'd have made coffee."

He frowned as she carried his plate to the table for him. "I don't drink coffee."

"All right, then. Will the girls be up soon?"

"They're usually up by now."

"I'll get their pancakes ready, then." She walked back to the stove and continued cooking, while he took his seat.

As he ate, he wondered how on earth he was going to figure out how to woo her. Was it even possible?

The girls came down a few minutes later, and they were together. He had a feeling Amy had slept in Victoria's bed again. They'd done that a lot when one of them was upset since Marie had died.

"Did you sleep well?" he asked.

"I did," Amy said with a yawn. "I'm looking forward to learning to cook more today."

Caroline had breakfast for both of them on plates and carried it to the table. "I want to think about schooling starting on Monday. Today will be all about cooking." She looked at Andrew. "There is some food I'll need. Do you mind if I hitch up the wagon and drive to town?"

He shook his head. "I have an account at the store. Just let Mr. Snow know that you're my new wife."

Victoria smiled. "I want to go to town!"

Caroline nodded. "I'll take you both as soon as your beds are made and the breakfast dishes are done." She'd made her bed before coming out to fix breakfast.

Victoria's eyes narrowed. "You know I don't like making my bed."

"I do know. Do a good job, won't you?" Caroline brought her own plate to the table and sat down to eat, ignoring the glares from the older girl. It was time for her to assert her authority as the woman of the house. If Victoria wanted to go to town, she would obey.

Amy smiled. "I'll make Dad's bed for you, if you want, Caro—" She stopped mid-sentence. "Am I allowed to call you by your name?"

"Yes, of course. Call me Caroline. I know I'm not your mother."

"Thank you, Caroline. I'll make Dad's bed for you."

"That would be lovely. We'll plan on laundry on Monday, all right?"

Victoria curled her nose. "I don't do laundry."

"All right." *When her dresses walk around by themselves, she might change her mind.*

Andrew frowned at Caroline, worried she was giving Victoria too much leeway. "I'll have my girls carry their weight."

"Don't worry. They will." *Besides, you only want a glorified housekeeper anyway.*

Amy once again helped with the dishes, because she was excited to be the one to wash them. When they were finished, Caroline headed for the stairs. "I need to make sure beds are made so we can go into town."

Amy hurried up before her. "I'll get Dad's bed made."

"Thank you, Amy."

Caroline was already thrilled with the girl and how willing she was to do any task set before her, even volunteering for tasks. Caroline had been that way herself.

She peeked into Amy's room, and it was neat as a pin, just as Caroline had expected it to be.

Walking down the hall to Victoria's room, she found the girl sitting on the side of her bed, carefully braiding her hair. The bed was unmade, and there were clothes on her floor. "Oh, you don't want to go to town with us? We'll see you when we return, then."

Caroline turned and walked away, knowing it would infuriate Victoria, but the girl needed to have a better attitude. If she started out too soft with her, she knew that Victoria would walk all over her forever.

She walked down the stairs with Victoria chasing after her. "I do want to go!"

"You should have made your bed, then, Victoria. Next time perhaps you'll do as you're asked without having to be asked multiple times."

Victoria stared after her with a stunned expression. "You're really not going to let me go?"

"No, I'm really not." Caroline refused to back down.

Amy hurried down the stairs. "I'm ready to go, Caroline."

"Wonderful. Let's go get the wagon hitched up." Thankfully, Caroline had learned to do many chores like hitching up teams while she was helping at the orphanage. She wouldn't need to ask for help.

When she got outside, she saw that the team had already been hitched to the wagon, ready to go. She would need to give Andrew a mental point in the wooing game. Hitching the team up had been a big help to her, though she wasn't sure his actions were meant to be romantic.

She climbed into the wagon and picked up the leads, waiting as Amy climbed in beside her. "How do you like living in Whistle Stop?" she asked.

Amy smiled. "I do like it. We've always lived here, but until a couple of years ago, we lived in a small cabin on the ranch. Dad built this new one just before Mom died."

"I'm very sorry about your mother. I know how hard it is to lose someone you love so much."

"Thank you." Amy looked straight ahead for a moment. "Do you think it would hurt my mom if she knew that I liked you?"

"I don't think so at all. If it were me and I'd lost my daughter, I would want them to be happy. Right now, Victoria isn't happy, and she isn't going to be happy until she settles down and starts doing what's asked of her. Your mom would probably be very unhappy with that."

Amy thought about it for a moment before nodding. "Mom would hate to see Victoria act like she has been. She'd be angry with me for the way I acted with the housekeepers too, though."

"Did you help your sister with pranks?"

Amy nodded. "I did. And I deliberately didn't help around the house, even though I wanted to. It's not like me to be slothful, but

Victoria said it's what the housekeepers deserved because they were trying to take Mom's place."

"No one can take your mom's place, but I've found that the more people I love, the more love I have in my heart. So why would I deny someone love just because they are doing the job of someone else I loved?"

When they got to town, they did some shopping, and Caroline let Amy help her choose what she would make that week for meals. When it was time to check out, she introduced herself to Mr. Snow. "I'm Mrs. Caroline Dawson. My husband told me to just put whatever I purchase today on his account."

Mr. Snow smiled and nodded. "I guess you're the mail-order bride he had me telegraph about."

"I am." Caroline felt very adventurous being called a mail-order bride. She knew some women would look down on her for the way she'd found her husband, but she really didn't care. They hadn't had the courage to take a train across the country all alone to marry a stranger.

"We're happy to have you here in Whistle Stop, then. Someday, you'll have to meet my wife."

"Oh, I'd like that. Will you be at church tomorrow?"

"Everyone in town will be in church tomorrow, Mrs. Dawson. You can meet her then."

"I would be grateful for an introduction, Mr. Snow."

"Let me have my boy carry your purchases to your wagon."

That's when Caroline realized the appeal of going to town for Victoria. The Snow boy was about fourteen and a handsome young man. Well, no wonder Victoria was angry she hadn't been allowed to go to the store with them.

"Thank you for your help, Mr. Snow." Caroline nodded to the boy. As they drove back toward the ranch, Caroline asked, "How long has Victoria had a crush on the Snow boy?"

Amy giggled. "Joshua? Always. I think she was born with a crush."

"She's going to be very angry that we actually went to the store without her, then, isn't she?"

Amy nodded emphatically. "Oh, yes. Madder than a hornet."

"That's going to be interesting." Caroline wasn't afraid of the girl, and she wasn't worried about what would happen. She was very intrigued by the situation, though, and she now knew how to make the girl behave. Twice weekly trips to town could easily be taken . . . for the right behavior.

When they arrived home, Victoria was sitting at the table in the kitchen, and she glared at them both. "Victoria, I would appreciate your help carrying the supplies we purchased inside."

"No." The one-syllable word was drawn out and used as a taunt.

"Oh, all right. I was just thinking you'd want to attend church tomorrow, but until I can be sure that you'll act the way you should in public, I'm afraid you're going to have to be confined to the house." Caroline said the words off-handedly, as if they meant nothing, but they were her answer to all of the juvenile behavior she'd been subject to since her arrival.

Victoria gasped and jumped to her feet. "You can't do that! Dad won't let you!"

"Oh, I'm afraid your father has told me that I have free rein when it comes to disciplining you girls. He has no idea what to do with you anymore." Though she was stretching the truth a bit, it didn't bother Caroline at all. She wasn't about to put up with any more of the girl's attitude if it could be helped.

"But . . . I have to be able to go to town."

Caroline straightened up and looked straight into Victoria's eyes. The girl was tall, and only a couple of inches shorter than she was. "The choice is yours, Victoria. You behave, and you can go to town whenever I go. You don't behave, and you'll be in the house at all times."

Victoria seemed as if she was having an internal argument, but then she walked slowly toward the wagon. "I'll help, but I won't like it."

"I'm not asking for you to enjoy it. For now, simple obedience is my goal." Caroline continued carrying in supplies with the girls, and when they were done, she unhitched the team. "I'd like you both to work on putting things away while I get this done."

Both girls went inside to help, and when Caroline had the horses in their pasture and she was back in the house, she found that everything had been put away to her satisfaction. "Wonderful. Thank you, girls."

She sat for a minute with a glass of water before jumping up. "I want us to get the house completely cleaned and company ready today. Tomorrow is church, and then Monday we'll do laundry. Then Tuesday, I want us to put in a kitchen garden. We can also plant some flowers near the front steps. I think they'll look lovely."

"Mom planned to do that," Amy said softly.

"Well, then we'll have to plant her favorite flowers to honor her memory," Caroline said.

Victoria said nothing, but the anger on her face spoke volumes.

Chapter Four

THEY BAKED SEVERAL loaves of bread that day as well as making supper and cake for dessert. Both girls helped Caroline, though Victoria grumbled more than her share. Amy did it all with a smile, singing along with Caroline.

After the cake and bread were baked, Caroline sat at the table with both girls. "Now we need to clean the windows, which is the absolute worst part of housekeeping. So I will do the outside of the windows if you girls will do the inside."

"And upstairs?" Amy asked.

"I'm not worried about doing the outside of the upstairs. Just the inside."

Victoria once again had a bad attitude, but this time she did as she was asked the first time, splitting the windows with her sister.

By the time Andrew walked into the house that afternoon, everything sparkled. The laundry was the only thing left, and that would be conquered on Monday.

Amy set the table while Victoria carried the serving dishes to the table and Caroline spread whipped cream on the top of the cake they'd baked.

Andrew stopped for a moment, watching the three ladies in his life flutter around in unison. He wondered what Caroline had done to get Victoria to do as she was told, but he would wait until later to ask her.

He walked to his wife and kissed her forehead, presenting her with the flowers he'd picked. He wouldn't tell her he hadn't thought of it until he was on his way back at the end of the day. She wanted to be courted, and he would do his best, though he was more than a little rusty.

She accepted the flowers with a smile, walking over to take the wilted ones from the previous day out of the vase and replace them with the fresh ones. "Thank you, Andrew."

Victoria glared at her father. "You never brought Mom flowers."

He started to tell her that was because her mother was sleeping in his bed every night without flowers, but he bit his tongue. "I took your mother flowers before you were born." And he had. Twice. Before they'd married as well.

Victoria still didn't seem happy with her father, but she said nothing else as she plopped down at the table while Caroline filled the glasses with milk. "How was your day?" Caroline asked.

"It was a day. A couple of the men are out with a stomach bug so those of us left were doing the job of two men. It's calving season, and we're busier than any man ought to be."

"Calves? I want to see the calves."

Victoria sneered at Caroline. "They look just like regular cows, but they're smaller."

Caroline smiled sweetly. "I'm sure they do, but I still want to see them."

"There's one that we're trying to get another heifer to feed. He lost his mother. If she won't accept him, I may bring him to you to be bottle fed."

Caroline clapped her hands in enthusiasm. "Oh, I would adore that! Wouldn't you, girls?"

Victoria didn't respond and took a bite of her supper instead. Amy smiled and nodded. "I would love to help with that."

Andrew was pleased at the easy camaraderie between his new wife and his younger daughter, but Victoria was another story. He wasn't sure why she was so filled with hate, but she needed to be kinder to her new stepmother. "How did shopping go?"

"Oh, it was really nice. Mr. Snow's kind son carried our supplies to the wagon for us. He's a handsome young man, isn't he?" Caroline made sure not to look at Victoria as she said the words, because she didn't want the girl to know she'd found her weakness.

"Joshua? He's a good boy. I'm glad you had help. Supper is wonderful, and the house looks great. I can't believe how hard you three have been working."

It was more like two and a half people working, but Caroline was happy for the half from Victoria. She'd win her over yet. "I'm glad you're pleased. What time do we leave for church in the morning?"

"Services are at eleven, so we usually leave around ten fifteen. It gives the girls some time to talk to their friends before the service starts." He took a big drink of his milk, thankful there was hot food on the table every night again. After a little wooing, perhaps there would be a warm willing body in his bed once more as well.

"That sounds good. Do you have chores to do before church, or should I plan a late breakfast?"

"I need to do some chores. I need to check on that calf who may need to be bottle fed and do the milking. I would say we can have breakfast a little late, but no later than six thirty or so."

"Sounds good to me."

After supper, Caroline stood to clear the table. "I'm going to wash again," Amy said with a grin.

"Then you'll wipe the dishes, Victoria. Your new mother should have some time to sit with me and talk."

Victoria glared at Caroline, but she did as she was told.

Caroline smiled sweetly at the girl. "Thank you, girls."

Andrew took Caroline's hand. "Let's go into the parlor."

She followed him, happy to spend a little time with him. She was ready to see what he thought courting involved.

"Victoria is a lot more obedient today than yesterday, I see," he said to her. "What did you do?"

Caroline smiled. "She didn't make her bed this morning, so I didn't let her go into town with us."

"Oh!"

"And that's where I learned what motivates her. She didn't want to help unload the wagon, and I told her she couldn't go to church tomorrow unless she did."

He chuckled. "That Snow boy still have her eye?"

"According to Amy he does. Either way, she doesn't want to have to be on the ranch all the time, so she's acting as she should." Caroline smiled at him. "I hope you're all right with me making those threats."

"Absolutely. You do what you need to do to make that girl behave." He shook his head. "I know I've been too soft on both of them since they lost their mother. Victoria used to get into screaming fights with Marie because she didn't get her way, but Marie never backed down. I wasn't involved in their lives much before she died, and it's odd for me to be so involved now. I feel like I'm drowning every time they look at me with tears in their eyes."

Caroline shook her head. "I can't allow them to disobey. Victoria is obeying everything I say because of the threats, but she's stomping around and glaring at me a great deal."

"And you're satisfied with that?"

"I am. It'll only get better. I feel like I have to start out firm. I can be easier later, but the firmer I am now, the better it will be later."

He nodded. "I bow to your expertise in this. Did you have younger siblings?"

"No," she said. "I cooked at an orphanage. I was a volunteer, and I spent as much time with the children as I could. I learned a lot about being a homemaker there."

"Not from your own mother?"

"I lost my mother when I was around Victoria's age, and I got a new stepmother. I remember hating her with everything inside me, but she was kind, and she eventually won me over. I was an only child, and I'm sure I threw more fits than any child ever had the right to."

"At least you're not surprised by it, then." He shook his head. "The girls hated all the housekeepers I brought in as well."

"Amy told me about that. She said they 'ghosted' the last one. I know I finished cleaning up the flour from their little prank."

"Did she tell you why?"

"She said they were afraid the housekeepers would try to take their mother's place. All of this is about people trying to be their mother." She sighed. "Amy has been absolutely lovely. And I will get through to Victoria. I promise you that."

"There's no doubt in my mind," Andrew said with a grin. He'd never met anyone quite like his new wife. "You're a pretty amazing woman, Caroline."

She smiled. "I think so. And I will continue to be. Trust me, the girls and I are doing fine. They won't ghost me."

"I'm glad." He brought one hand to her cheek. "I'm very sorry I rejected you last night. I hope it didn't ruin the day for you."

Caroline grinned. "I still had my perfect wedding day, just not my perfect wedding night. Eventually we'll have that, when you've wooed me sufficiently." She felt the need to let him know she hadn't forgotten about her edict.

He groaned. "I was hoping the flowers would be considered sufficient."

She laughed. "Not even close. You made your bed, and now you have to lie in it."

"I'd be more comfortable if you'd lie in it with me."

She shook her head. "You've only kissed me one time, and that was because I forced it. You suddenly talk like you want me in your bed, but you certainly don't act like it."

"I wasn't sure of your wooing rules and if I was allowed to kiss you before sufficient wooing had occurred. Are you sure we can't just pretend last night never happened and declare tonight our wedding night?"

"Absolutely positive. You had ten minutes to reverse your silly decision, and you stuck to it. Now you get to make me feel loved before you get to touch me that way." She shrugged. "Maybe you'll think before you say silly things in the future."

He sighed, putting his hands on her shoulders and pulling her to him. "What if I kiss you so much that you beg me to take you to bed with me?"

"Then you win. For now, you have to show me that you deserve to win." She winked at him, happy to play this game with him. She was glad he was a man she felt perfectly at ease with, because it made teasing him this way so much easier. And she did love to tease.

"So that means that when I finally do get you in bed, I win?"

"I think I'd call that both of us winning, wouldn't you?" Caroline looked at him through her lashes, trying to be playful. She had no idea how she was supposed to act with a man she was married to, so she followed her instincts.

He leaned down and pressed his lips to hers, softly at first before deepening the kiss. He softly traced her lips with his tongue, and she opened for him, gasping softly when his tongue entered her mouth. She'd been kissed a few times back in Beckham but never like this.

Her arms went around his neck, and she let out a small sigh as she moved closer to him. What she really wanted to do was climb onto his lap, but she didn't have the courage to be quite so forward.

"Dad I—" The voice suddenly stopped. "How could you? What about Mom?" Victoria ran off, sobbing.

Caroline felt his arms and mouth move away from her, and then he was running after Victoria. She buried her face in her hands and took deep breaths. The man could kiss. There was no doubt about that. She hoped she was able to keep her resolve and wait until he was ready to show her how much she meant to him.

She waited for what seemed an eternity for him to come back, and when he didn't, she went off to bed, once more reading *Jane Eyre*.

Rochester, though a strange hero to be certain, was someone she could love. Any woman could. She hoped that Andrew would—in time—become her Rochester.

CHURCH THE FOLLOWING morning was interesting for Caroline. Having always lived in Beckham, while not a large city, it was certainly much larger than Whistle Stop. The church services were small, and everyone seemed to know one another. She met several different ladies, a few of whom were her age. Many were older. And she watched the girls.

There were few girls their age, but they gravitated to the ones who were there, and they all watched Joshua Snow. Every single girl there seemed to have a crush on the boy, and they all seemed fine with the others having the same crush.

For his part, Joshua seemed completely oblivious of the others. It was funny to watch everything unfold, knowing how strongly Victoria felt for the boy.

To his credit, Andrew remained at Caroline's side before and after the service, introducing her as his new wife to everyone who came by. Caroline felt as if she was under a magnifying glass as everyone looked her up and down and asked about her background.

Many of the people she met were kind to her, and they all seemed welcoming. She talked to Amanda, who said she had been a close friend of Marie's. She promised to come over for tea one day that week. "Any idea what day?" Caroline asked. She didn't want to be digging in the dirt when a new friend came to visit.

Amanda shrugged. "Why don't we plan on Thursday? Would that work for you?"

"Yes, it would. The girls and I are going to be planting a kitchen garden and flowers around the house this week, and I didn't want to be covered in dirt when you stopped by."

"I wouldn't mind as long as you let me make the tea!" Amanda said with a smile. "How are you getting along with the girls?"

Caroline smiled. "Amy and I are already fast friends. Victoria and I have come to an agreement, and she's learning to be obedient."

"That's more than her mother was ever able to do with her. The girl has always been a difficult one to be around."

"And now she talks as if she worshiped her mother and I'm a horrible person and trying to take her place."

Amanda frowned. "I'm not surprised at all." She patted Caroline's arm. "We'll talk when I come over."

"Thank you. I could use advice from someone who knows her better than I do."

Amanda left soon after with her husband and three daughters, leaving Caroline to expel a breath. "That was interesting. So many new people to meet."

Andrew nodded. "They are all glad you're here, though. Everyone thinks someone needs to take Victoria in hand." He loved his daughter dearly, but he knew she was a problem. It had seemed like Amy was following in her footsteps, but he could clearly see now that wasn't the case.

"So will you work today?" Caroline asked as they all walked out to the wagon together.

He shook his head. "No, I only do necessary chores on Sundays. I try to keep the Sabbath and spend the day with my girls."

"That sounds fun. Perhaps we could all go for a walk this afternoon, and you could show me the ranch and the area around it."

"Do you ride?" he asked.

"No, that's one skill I have yet to learn. Perhaps you could teach me?"

"Not today, though. Let's go home and have some lunch, and then we'll spend the afternoon exploring the countryside." He helped Caroline into the wagon before looking at the girls. "What do you say?"

Amy nodded eagerly, but Victoria gave her usual frown. Caroline wished there was something she could do to help the girl to be happier, but she had no idea at all what could do that.

"What do you have planned for the week?" Andrew asked as they drove toward the house. He'd learned that asking her questions kept her talking and he had to contribute little to the conversation, which was exactly how he liked it.

"The girls and I are doing laundry tomorrow," Caroline said.

"I'm not!" Victoria said. "I told you I hate laundry, and I *won't* do it."

"That's too bad. I guess Amy and I will have to go into town to buy seeds alone on Tuesday morning." Caroline turned back to Andrew. "Tuesday we're going to plant a kitchen garden, and I hope to plant some flowers for the front of the house. I think it will brighten up the whole yard."

"You can't go into town without me again. Dad, tell her she has to take me!" Victoria demanded.

Andrew thought about the best way to phrase what he needed to say. "If you help with the laundry tomorrow and do everything else you are told to do, then I think you'll be able to go to town on Tuesday. If you don't, I think you should be left behind."

"You can't take her side against your own daughter!"

"I can and I have."

"We're also going to start some schoolwork tomorrow," Caroline added as if nothing had just happened. She refused to give much attention to Victoria's outbursts. She was sure that was what the girl wanted.

"Really? Do you feel qualified to teach them?"

Caroline nodded emphatically. "I graduated from school, so I'm perfectly capable. I even helped teach the orphans at times."

"Then I'm glad you'll be giving some attention to their studies." He pulled up in front of the house. He was surprised that Victoria had stopped complaining, but he was glad she had. Perhaps his new wife understood his daughter better than he did. She certainly seemed to be having greater luck with her. "Let's have our lunch, and then we'll go for that walk. Maybe I'll even hold your hand and pick some flowers for you," he said as he helped Caroline down from the wagon.

"I guess you're not a total loss at wooing after all."

Chapter Five

AFTER THEY FINISHED the lunch dishes, the family of four set out on their Sunday afternoon walk. Victoria lagged behind, but Amy stayed right with Andrew and Caroline. Amy happily talked about different things that had happened throughout the time Caroline was there. She truly seemed to be overjoyed to have her new stepmother.

True to his word, Andrew held Caroline's hand as they walked, and he pointed out different things of note. He showed her the mesquite trees and a large field of bluebonnets.

Amy picked some and then ran to catch up. "I want to give these to you, Caroline. Thank you."

Caroline stopped walking and looked at Amy. "For what?" She noted that Victoria was still out of earshot.

"For being kind to me. You're nothing like the stepmother in *Cinderella*."

Caroline laughed, embracing the girl. "I try not to be like her."

Victoria glared at them as the flowers were exchanged, but she said nothing. She obviously wanted no part of being with the others.

When they resumed their walk, Amy hurried back to her sister and whispered something, but she was soon back with her father and Caroline. "Victoria is not happy that I like you, Caroline," she said softly.

Caroline frowned. "Well, I'm glad you like me. It's nice to have someone to talk to during the day while your dad is working."

"I'm glad you're teaching me so much. I'd never kneaded bread until yesterday. It's much harder work than I thought it would be." Amy seemed to be thrilled that she was learning to work harder.

"Wait until we churn our own butter," Caroline said with a grin. Having been raised in town, she had never had to churn butter until she started helping out with the orphans. They were as self-sufficient as they could possibly be there, so they had used the cream from the cows there on the property to make the butter. She had grown to enjoy the laborious task.

"Oh, when will we do that? Mom had a butter churn she used a lot, but I think someone put it in the spare room."

"Yes, it's in the room where I'm staying. We'll do it later in the week. I'm sure the housekeepers churned their own butter."

Amy shook her head. "All the housekeepers cared about was cooking and doing a little cleaning. If they could buy anything at all at the store, they would. They didn't care about saving money."

"Well, I care about saving money. If you decide you want to go off to medical school in a few years, we can pay for at least part of it with the money we save from churning our own butter."

Andrew smiled at that. Caroline had no idea how much money he had, and he was happy to keep it that way. The ranch was large and doing well. There was no need to scrimp in any way, but if it made her feel like she was contributing, then he was all for it. "Are you planning to go to medical school, Amy?"

"Nope. I'm going to marry Josh and have a dozen children and help him run his father's store."

Caroline gasped. "You have a crush on the same boy your sister does?"

"Not at all. He's just the most appealing boy in town, so I've decided he should be mine." The grin on the girl's face told Caroline she was joking.

"Well, if you do have a dozen children, I'd be happy to play grandmother. I do love children." Caroline worried after the words had escaped her mouth that they might be misconstrued as her trying to take the place of Marie, and she held her breath until Amy responded.

"I'd like that a lot. You can watch them while I go dancing with my husband."

Caroline looked at Andrew. "Is there a place to dance in town?"

"Of course not. We have barn dances sometimes, but that's about it. She's being silly." Andrew shook his head, but there was a grin on his face.

"Maybe by the time I'm married, there will be a place to dance. I'm sure someone will open something like that someday."

"Not in Whistle Stop."

Amy shrugged. "A girl can dream, and if I'm going to dream, I'm going to dream big."

"I like to say that if you don't reach for the stars, you'll never make it to the moon. I know it's silly, but I like the idea of dreaming big." Caroline glanced over her shoulder to see that Victoria was almost out of sight she was lagging so far behind. "I'm going to go and try to talk to Victoria."

Andrew frowned for a moment but finally nodded. "That's probably a good idea."

"I think it is." Caroline turned and walked back to the girl, smiling at her. "Are you enjoying our walk?"

Victoria kicked a clump of dirt on their path. "You're not my mom."

Caroline wasn't sure she could count how many times the girl had said that in the short while she'd been in Texas. "No, I'm not. And I'm not trying to be. I just want to be a friend who happens to be married to your father."

"I don't want you here."

"I can see that. What I don't understand is why. I'm going to make your life easier by being here."

Victoria glared at her. "How do you think you're going to do that?"

"I'm a woman, just like you are. When you need to talk about something important and your father doesn't know how to talk about it, you'll be glad I'm here. In the meantime, I'm just going to keep doing what I'm doing. You're not going to be able to get rid of me like you did the housekeepers."

The smile on Victoria's face was obviously mischievous. "You don't think?"

"No, I really don't. I don't scare easily, and I'm happy here. I like Texas a great deal more than I thought I would." Caroline was exaggerating a bit, but she knew she'd be happy as soon as she could make her husband fall in love with her. And it was going to happen. "Why don't you hurry with me and walk with the rest of us. We're having fun."

"No thank you. I'm happier back here where I can't hear you."

Caroline shook her head. "Suit yourself." She hurried to rejoin Amy and Andrew, her hand automatically sliding into her husband's. "She doesn't want to walk with us. Her loss."

Andrew frowned. "I don't know how to make her be kinder to you."

"You don't need to. Victoria and I will work through it. I promise."

"All right. That works for me." Andrew truly didn't want to feel like he had to choose between his daughter and his new wife.

"I felt very strongly that my stepmother was trying to take my mother's place when she first married my father. Now we're extremely close. I really do understand why Victoria is upset."

Amy frowned. "She didn't get along with Mom either. She was always yelling at her."

Caroline was surprised to hear Amy confirm what she'd already been told. Not surprised that it was true, but surprised that Amy would admit it. "Maybe she's happier when she yells."

Andrew tried to keep a straight face, but then he started to laugh softly. It didn't take long before his laughter was full blown, and he had to stop walking to laugh.

Caroline and Amy just looked at him as if he'd lost his mind. "Are you all right?" Caroline finally asked.

He shook his head, trying to stop. "I *really do* think she's happier yelling," he said, and then he started laughing again. No one had ever said anything quite so true. Victoria had been a yeller since the moment she was born.

"Why is that funny?" Caroline asked Amy.

"I don't know. But she does yell *a lot*."

Caroline was starting to worry about her husband. His face was turning red, and he didn't seem to be in control. "Should we head back?"

Finally, Andrew shook his head and got his laughter under control. "I don't think anyone in the world is happier yelling except my darling daughter."

"We'll help her. I promise." Caroline could still see the sadness in Victoria's eyes, and she felt badly for her. She didn't understand what had tickled Andrew so much, but she was glad that he seemed to be under control again.

"I believe in you," Andrew said, taking her hand again.

"Does she yell at you, Amy?" Caroline asked, suddenly wondering how the younger sister was able to deal so well with the older.

"She more whisper yells. She doesn't want anyone to know she's yelling at me and telling me what to do, but her whispers feel like yells." Amy glanced over her shoulder to make sure Victoria hadn't caught up with them. "She scares me sometimes."

"I can see that." Caroline frowned. "Let me know if she gets out of control, please."

"I will. I promise."

Caroline didn't have a very good sense of direction, so she was surprised when their walk took them back around to the house. She looked around her. "How did we get back here?"

Andrew grinned. "I think my wife may need to learn how to navigate this ranch."

"Maybe I do." She shrugged. "I think I'm going to put a stew on for supper if that sounds good."

"Anything you cook sounds good to me."

Caroline looked at Amy. "Are you good at peeling potatoes?"

"I've never done it."

"Really? I'll teach you." Caroline put her arm around Amy and ushered her inside, stopping at the door. "Victoria, Amy and I are making stew for supper. Would you like to help us?" She was determined to make Victoria feel like she was always welcome to do whatever she was doing, whether the girl accepted or not.

"Only if I'm required to do it."

"You can do whatever you want." Caroline knew it would go better without the sullen girl's help.

"I'll go to my room, then."

Caroline shrugged, looking at Amy after Victoria had disappeared. "What does she *do* up there all day?"

"No idea. She doesn't like to read at all. I think she mostly just talks to herself." Amy looked as if she'd never thought about what her sister did all day, but she knew it was odd that she disappeared for so long.

"Okay, let's learn to peel potatoes and carrots." Caroline demonstrated and smiled as Amy caught on so quickly. The girl was an absolute joy to be around.

Andrew sat at the table, whittling a small animal. He had an entire collection that he thought he would give to a son one day, but . . . only his daughters had survived. Perhaps that would change now that he was married again. A thought popped into his mind, and he smiled. He knew of a good way to woo his sweet wife.

AFTER THE GIRLS WERE in bed that evening, Andrew led Caroline into the parlor. "I thought we could spend a little time together."

Caroline smiled. "Time is all I ever ask for."

"Time and wooing."

"Well, with as busy as you are, spending time with me *is* wooing."

He smiled, reaching into the pocket on his shirt and pulling out a tiny carved bunny. "This is for you."

She took it from him, turning it over and over in her hand and smiling with pleasure. "I love it."

"I have an entire forest full of animals carved. I always thought I'd give them to my son, if I ever had one."

"We'll have a son together," she said softly.

"*After* I woo you properly."

"I will say that the flowers were a good start. And then our walk today was absolutely lovely. I enjoyed church and meeting everyone. Amanda is coming for tea, and I'm looking forward to getting to know her."

"I'm glad you liked the service, and I really hope that you and Amanda get along well." His face was skeptical as he leaned back on the sofa, wrapping an arm around her shoulders. "So is kissing a good part of wooing?"

She laughed. "I like your kisses a lot, so yes, they're part of wooing."

"Good. Because all day when we were at church and with the girls, all I could think of was kissing you."

"Really?"

He nodded, taking her shoulders in his hands and pulling her toward him. "Really." He lowered his lips to hers and kissed her softly. This sweet woman he'd married was changing his world one day at a time. He'd expected to have her arrive and treat her like he had the different housekeepers he'd hired, but she was special.

His kiss surprised Caroline, because this time was much more intense than the other occasions when he'd kissed her. His lips toyed with hers, and he deepened the kiss. When he lifted his head, she wanted to bring his mouth back to hers. She felt almost bereft without it.

"How are your kisses so intoxicating? When boys tried to kiss me back home, all I wanted was for them to go away. You kiss me, and I want to crawl inside your clothing with you."

He grinned. "I like that idea. Maybe you want to crawl into my bed with me?"

She tilted her head to one side, considering his question. She'd thought she would make him wait for months for the physical side of their marriage, but all at once, she didn't want to. She was punishing herself as well as him by making him wait.

After a long moment, where he all but held his breath waiting for her response, she nodded. "I'd like that a lot."

"You would? Really?" Andrew hadn't expected her to agree so readily. He'd expected to be tormented by her for at least a month.

She laughed. "Really."

"I'll give you ten minutes to ready yourself for bed, and then I'll join you."

Her heart was in her throat as she got her nightgown from the room she'd been using and took it upstairs, changing in the dark. She was well aware of his girls just down the hall and hoped neither of them would wake up and come out of their rooms. She was sure Victoria would be very angry to find Caroline in her father's room.

She slipped between the covers, promising herself she would wash all the linens with the rest of the clothes the next day. Her mind was always filled with the next task, but she hoped she could free it to concentrate on her husband for the next little while.

Her stepmother had carefully explained what would happen between her and her husband, and though the very idea had been a little embarrassing and frightening, more than anything it had been exciting. She was ready for this next step with Andrew.

He opened the door and undressed in the dark, looking at the bed and realizing he could just make out her figure there under the covers. It had been so long since he'd been with a woman, he was worried he'd hurry too quickly and frighten her. He took deep even breaths, trying to tell himself that slowly was good with his innocent wife.

He slipped under the covers with her, reaching for her. When she came across the bed and snuggled up against him as if they'd been making love for years, he was surprised but pleased.

He cupped her face in his hands, kissing her passionately. His hands roamed over her body through her nightgown, and he wondered how she'd feel if he took it off. He decided to just do it and stop wondering, unbuttoning the three buttons at the neck of her white nightgown and pushing the V it made wide, so he could kiss her chest.

His hand came up to cup her breast, and she gasped softly. "I didn't think you'd touch me there," she said softly.

"I plan on touching you everywhere."

"Is that all right?" Her stepmother had told her the basics of what would happen, but she'd said nothing of the pleasure that touching before the actual marital act could bring. She was happy he was experienced enough to know what to do, because she truly had no clue.

He nodded. "We're married. Any way we want to touch each other is fine."

"It is?"

"Yes, it is."

She knew he wasn't wearing anything, so her hand went to the part of him she was curious about, and he groaned.

"I'm not sure I'm ready for you to touch me *there.*"

"But you said it was fine!" She jerked her hand away, worried she'd done something wrong.

"It is fine, but if you touch me there, everything is going to happen too quickly. I want this first time to be good for you."

She had no idea why her touching him there would make it go faster, but she knew he understood what they were doing better than she did. She moved her hands to his shoulders instead, gently stroking them. "Is that better?"

"Much." Truly, he wanted her hand where she'd put it first, but it wouldn't be good for her first experience if she kept touching him there.

When he finally covered her body with his, she wrapped her arms around him and held tight, feeling first pain, but then pleasure as he moved within her.

When he had again rolled to his side, she rested her cheek against his shoulder. "Will we do that often?" she asked softly.

He chuckled. "I think we will."

"Oh, good. It made me feel very close to you. And it felt . . . well, it felt good. I didn't know it was supposed to feel good."

"God made our bodies to fit together in a way that would always feel good. Never think that anything we can do together in our bed is wrong."

She grinned. "Can I touch you there now?"

He chuckled. "Now's probably a good time. There's nothing to speed up at this point."

They lay there in the dark, exploring one another's bodies for a long while. Each of them pleased to have found someone they could feel free with.

Chapter Six

MONDAY WAS AN EXERCISE in patience for Caroline. She was up before everyone as usual and had breakfast made before anyone else joined her in the kitchen. As everyone ate their scrambled eggs and toast, she told the girls she needed all dirty clothes downstairs immediately after breakfast.

Amy nodded, but Victoria ignored her.

After Andrew was gone for the day, Caroline washed the dishes, and after bringing down the dirty clothes, Amy wiped them for her. "Where's Victoria?" Caroline asked.

"She said she hates laundry, and she's not going to help."

Caroline nodded. "I'll talk with her once we're finished here."

Amy nodded. "I wasn't sure if you wanted me to get Dad's dirty clothes."

"No, I'll do that. Are you going to help me do the wash today?"

"Yes. Mom never thought I was old enough to help, but I always wanted to."

"You like cleaning, don't you?"

Amy grinned. "It was always my favorite thing to do. I know it's silly, but why not do it when I enjoy it?"

"I never did any housework growing up. We always had a maid. But then I started working at the orphanage, and I discovered that I love to cook and clean. I am doing just the right thing by being in an area where I have to do things for myself." Caroline washed the last dish and handed it to Amy. "I'm going to set the two of you up with schoolwork as soon as I have the laundry on the line."

"I want to help hang it on the line!"

Caroline grinned. "You know, if I didn't know better, I would think you were just trying to avoid schoolwork."

Amy shrugged. "I like to read. I'm not a fan of arithmetic."

"We'll make you a fan of arithmetic, too! Why don't you put a huge pot of water on to boil while I go upstairs and talk to your sister and gather laundry?"

Amy nodded, jumping to do as she was told.

Caroline dreaded the conversation she was going to have to have with Victoria, but there was no helping it. She couldn't allow the girl to keep disrespecting her the way she was. She knocked on her door before opening it. "Victoria, I need your dirty clothes, so I can do the laundry. Would you carry them downstairs please?"

"No, I don't think I will."

"That's fine. But remember if you don't help bring clothes down, you won't have any clean clothes to wear." Caroline turned away to go to Andrew's room—well their room now—to get his dirty clothes and sheets.

Victoria followed her out into the hallway. "Are you telling me that you won't do my laundry if I don't help?"

"That's exactly what I'm saying. I'm not the housekeeper. I'm the new stepmother. I'm willing to work beside you, but I won't work while you sit in your room and stare at the walls. If you like to have clean clothing, you'll help make them clean." Caroline didn't pause as she went into the master bedroom to gather the dirty laundry from it.

After hearing Victoria's door slam, she shook her head but continued with her work. She wasn't about to beat the girl, no matter how much she needed it. She was determined to be a good mother to both girls.

Once she got downstairs with all the clothes, she went into her little bedroom off the kitchen to gather her dirty laundry from there, and she saw that Amy had already done it for her. As difficult as Victoria was, Amy was just that sweet and helpful.

Caroline and Amy laughed and sang as they worked, enjoying themselves immensely, because they did it together. Just as they were hanging the clothes on the line, Victoria came down with an armload of clothes. "I need to have clean clothes to go into town tomorrow."

Amy grinned at Caroline. "I'll show you how to wash them Victoria."

Caroline listened as Amy quoted her almost word for word on how to wash the clothes. She continued hanging the clean clothes on the line, and then she helped the girls hang Victoria's clothes.

When everything was hanging to dry, Caroline said, "Let's go get you started on school. I can do the daily baking while you work on your lessons."

Victoria crossed her arms over her chest. "Why would I need to do schoolwork when I'm going to be a housewife? I just need to know how to cook and clean."

"You need to do the schoolwork if you want to be able to go into town. I thought we'd established that you'd be obedient or lose privileges." Caroline walked into the house and went straight to the pantry, where she pulled out the ingredients she needed to bake bread. She found that the whole family loved to eat the fresh bread she made, and it didn't last long.

The girls got their schoolbooks, but neither of them remembered where they were in their studies. Caroline had them read different things aloud and work on different arithmetic problems until she found where they should start. "There, now you girls study while I work on baking bread. Should we have a cake, a pie, or cookies for dessert tonight?"

Victoria didn't respond, but Amy suggested, "Pie!"

"What kind of pie? Do you have a favorite? I saw some dried apple in the pantry."

"I love apple pie!" Amy grinned.

"Then apple pie it will be."

The girls were mostly quiet as they worked, and Caroline made up three loaves of bread and an apple pie.

When it was time for lunch, they had sandwiches made from the bread she'd just baked. "I think doing school in the morning will be enough every day. I'm going to churn butter this afternoon."

Amy clapped her hands together excitedly. "I can't wait!"

"I'll be in my room," Victoria said.

"That's fine. I'll send Amy up to get you when it's time for you to help make supper."

Victoria wrinkled her nose and stomped off, letting everyone see what she thought of having to help fix supper.

Caroline and Amy churned butter together, and it wasn't long before Amy was complaining of the pain in her arms from doing the motions she was making with the churn. "Let me take a turn, then," Caroline said with a smile. This was going exactly as she'd expected.

When it was Amy's turn to churn the butter again, Caroline took the time to pack up her room and carry her things upstairs. If Amy noticed the move, she didn't say anything, which made things easier on Caroline.

Once the butter was in a nice ball, they put it into the ice box, and then talked about supper. After deciding what they would make, Caroline sent Amy up the stairs to fetch her sister to help. When Victoria was with them, Caroline took out a pencil and paper, and they made a list of what they wanted to get from the mercantile the next day.

Victoria didn't exactly participate in the shopping list discussion, but she didn't get up and leave, so Caroline decided it was a victory.

"Now that the shopping list is done, we need to bring in the laundry and fold it and put it away." Caroline loved how excited Amy seemed at the prospect and didn't allow herself to be annoyed by Victoria.

They brought in the clothes, and the three of them folded them all together. "Put your own clothes away, girls, and I'll put mine and your father's away."

When Victoria saw that Caroline was putting her own clothes in her father's room, she stopped for a moment and just glared at Caroline. "You're not making Dad forget Mom. You're not!"

"No one is going to forget your mother, Victoria. I'm just doing what I need to do as a new wife and stepmother." Caroline was calm as she put their things away. "I'm going to need help making the bed. Would you help me, Victoria? I'll help you with yours after."

Victoria seemed annoyed by the request, but she helped, and then Caroline helped her before moving on to help Amy with her bed. Once all three bedrooms looked bright and fresh, Caroline smiled. "I feel like we're mostly caught up on the housework now. Tomorrow we get to start planting! Only in the afternoon, though. I want you girls to devote your mornings to your studies."

Victoria wrinkled her nose, but Caroline didn't let herself care. She would find something in common with the girl, and they would become closer. She just knew it would work. "Your dresses are getting too short, Victoria. Have you had any new ones made since your mother passed?"

Victoria shook her head. "They're too tight here, too," Victoria said, pointing to the bodice. She seemed a little embarrassed when she said it, but Caroline just nodded, taking it in stride.

"I think it's time we passed those dresses down to Amy. I'll talk to your father tonight and see if he will let us pick out some pretty fabrics while we're in town tomorrow. I have a couple of patterns that I brought with me from back east. I bet we could size them to fit you perfectly."

Victoria looked at Caroline for a moment, her eyes narrowing. "Why are you being nice to me?"

"Because contrary to your beliefs, I'm a nice person. To everyone." Caroline wanted to shake the girl, but it would do no good. They'd work on her dresses, and then she'd make something pretty and new for Amy as well.

When Andrew got home, they had a nice pork roast on the table along with mashed potatoes and carrots. "This looks good enough to feed a king!" he said, wishing his girls weren't there and he could kiss his new wife. How did people ever have a second child, when the older ones were always there watching?

The girls did the supper dishes, and Victoria didn't even complain. Andrew pulled Caroline into the parlor. "Why didn't Victoria complain about doing the dishes? She always complains!"

"I told her I'd talk to you tonight about making her some new dresses. The ones she has are too short and getting tight in the bodice."

"I didn't even notice. Neither girl has had new dresses since Marie died. I guess it's time."

"I like to sew, and the girls need to learn. We'll make a lesson out of it and enjoy ourselves. Do you want to give me a budget? Amy can wear Victoria's hand-me-downs."

"There's no need for that," Andrew said, shaking his head. "If you don't mind sewing for them both, I think you'll find the girls will have *very* different color choices."

"That makes sense." While Amy was a blonde, her older sister was a redhead. Their coloring was different enough that they wouldn't look good in the same things. "You don't have a dollar amount in mind?"

"Do your best. I know you're frugal-minded, so you won't go crazy. I think two everyday dresses for each of the girls and one new church dress would be nice." He shrugged. "Do they need more than that?"

"Probably not. I want to make them both aprons as well. If they wear an apron every day, their dresses will stay cleaner."

"Sounds good to me. Whatever you think. Do they need new shoes?"

"I hadn't thought of that, but I'll look into it. They probably need all new undergarments and nightgowns as well." Caroline shook her head. "I'm going to be busy for a good long while."

"Do you mind?" he asked. He'd thought the housekeepers were keeping up with the girls' clothes, but obviously they hadn't been. There was so much for his new wife to do, he was worried she'd work herself into an early grave.

Caroline laughed. "Not at all. I like to stay busy. Sitting around with idle hands is not something I've ever enjoyed. While my friends were sitting around talking about boys, I was always knitting or darning socks or something. I couldn't just sit there."

He shook his head. "I guess I'm the same. Whenever I'm not doing anything else, I sit and whittle."

"I want to see what you've done."

"You saw the little rabbit I gave you."

She nodded. She'd put it on their dresser in their room. "I love that little rabbit."

He smiled. "I know. It got you into my bed." He winked at her.

She laughed, shaking her head. "No, if you'll remember, I was willing to sleep in your bed from my first night here. It was you who put it off."

"That's true . . ." He reached for her hand and pulled her to him, kissing her softly.

She heard a gasp and footsteps pounding as Victoria ran off again.

Caroline sighed, shaking her head. "She's going to get used to me. I promise."

"How did she act today? Did she help?"

"She did. At first, she told me she wasn't going to help with the laundry, but when I told her she would have to wear dirty clothes, she helped."

He laughed. "I like how you handle her. Marie had no idea what to do with such a headstrong child. She would cry to me every night."

"Victoria acts as if she resents me because I'm taking her mother's place, but knowing she acted the same with Marie tells me she just likes to be difficult."

Andrew shook his head. "I promise you, she was born that way. I'm just glad she's not dragging Amy into her little fits anymore."

"Amy was a little cold to me at first, but she and I are doing great. She loves to help. She helped me churn butter today, and her arms were aching." She sighed. "We washed all the bedding today as well. I'll do curtains next week. And tomorrow we're going to plant flowers. The girls started their schoolwork this morning, and they did it without too much complaining."

"I'm glad it's getting easier for you. After all the housekeepers we went through, I didn't think I'd ever find anyone who would be able to get through to the girls."

"I've made it clear to Victoria that no matter what, she can't get rid of me. I think that's helping."

Amy came into the room, then. "Victoria went upstairs crying and slammed her door."

"I know," Caroline said. "She'll be fine."

Amy smiled. "She *will* be fine. I'm going to go upstairs and see if she wants to talk."

"You do that."

As soon as Amy's footsteps were heard on the stairs, Andrew pulled Caroline close to him. "We're finally alone."

She laughed. "Were you waiting for them to leave?"

"I love my daughters, but at the moment, I want to love my new wife . . ."

"I think we need to wait until the girls are in bed for anything like you obviously have in mind."

"What exactly do you think I have in mind?" he asked.

She grinned. "Oh, probably lots more of what we did in bed last night." She'd expected to be embarrassed with him after they finally made love, but she wasn't. Not one little bit.

"You are a very astute woman . . ."

She leaned into him and kissed him softly. "I'm more than willing as soon as the girls are asleep."

"Why did I think it was a good idea to have children anyway?"

AS SOON AS THEY WERE finished with lunch the next day, Caroline took the girls out to the wagon for their drive to town. She hitched up the horses herself this time, carefully explaining what she was doing. She knew the girls weren't strong enough to hitch the team up alone, but she also felt like they should know how. If anything happened and they had to get to town quickly, they could work together to make it happen.

On the drive to town, they all three sat on the seat in the front of the wagon, Amy in the middle. "What color fabric do you want for your dresses?" Caroline asked them.

"How many do we get?" Victoria looked over at Caroline, excited about something for a change.

"We're going to start with two everyday dresses and one nice dress for each of you. And I'm going to make you aprons and new nightgowns as well."

"That's going to take a really long time to make," Victoria said.

Caroline shook her head. "No, I'm a fast seamstress, and I plan on teaching you girls to work with me. You can be doing some of the smaller seams while I work on other things. We'll get it all done together."

Victoria wrinkled her nose. "Mother never made us help make our own clothes."

"You were younger, then," Caroline responded. *And I'm not your mother, as you keep telling me.* "You're old enough to help now, and knowing how will help you later in life. We'll have fun doing it. I promise."

"Sewing is *not* fun." Victoria crossed her arms over her chest as she made the pronouncement.

"How do you know if you've never tried it?" Caroline asked.

Amy nodded. "Caroline makes everything fun. I even had fun churning butter, though my arms are sore today."

"They won't hurt as much next time. You'll learn that the more you do these things the easier they'll become."

"I'm only going to marry someone who has enough money to buy butter. Making it yourself is a waste of time," Victoria announced.

"I've never thought so, but you may have your own opinions." Caroline stopped the team in front of the mercantile. "Let's pick out our fabric first, and then we'll decide on what seeds we want to plant."

"Am I expected to help with the garden as well?" Victoria asked grumpily.

"Do you expect to eat?" Caroline answered with a smile.

Victoria made a face that immediately turned into a pretty smile. Caroline bit her lip. Joshua must be close.

"Hi, Joshua!" Victoria called out. "Would you mind helping me down?"

Caroline didn't watch, because she was afraid her face would betray her amusement. Victoria had scrambled into the wagon like a monkey, and now she needed help down? Taking Amy by the arm, Caroline headed into the mercantile for their shopping.

Chapter Seven

CAROLINE SAW MORE EXCITEMENT and enthusiasm on Victoria's face during that shopping trip than she had the rest of the time she'd been in Texas. The girl kept glancing over at Joshua, but she also applied herself to finding just the right fabric for her dresses. For her everyday dresses, she chose a mint green gingham as well as a flowered sky-blue fabric. And for her church dress, she chose a deep, rich purple with a tiny white flowered print on it.

She held it up in front of her, and nodded happily. "This one."

"I think those will all be lovely on you." Then Caroline turned to Amy. "Do you have any preferences?"

Amy shook her head. "I don't know what I want."

Victoria and Caroline exchanged a glance, and the two of them went to work, holding up different prints in front of Amy. Finally, they chose three different fabrics, and Caroline purchased some white linen for nightgowns and aprons as well as new petticoats and drawers for the girls.

They had two large boxes full by the time they bought the seeds and the food items they needed. "Is there a charity in town where we can donate the dresses the girls have outgrown?" Caroline asked at the counter. "I always gave my old dresses to an orphanage in town back in Massachusetts, but I have no idea what you have like that here."

"The church has a 'widows and orphans' room' where clothes are stored for anyone who may need them. Sometimes a fire will break out, and the family will be invited to go through whatever is there." Joshua volunteered the information as he picked up one of the boxes to take to the wagon.

"Thank you. I'll ask at the church on Sunday." Caroline smiled at Mr. Snow. "I do appreciate all your help."

"Happy to have your business, Mrs. Dawson."

On the drive home, Victoria seemed like a new girl. "Joshua took my hand and helped me down from the wagon," she told her sister.

Amy grinned. "Never wash your hand again!" She put the back of her hand against her forehead in a swooning motion as she said it, and Victoria made a face at her.

"When will we start sewing?" Victoria asked.

"We'll plant our seeds this afternoon and tomorrow afternoon. Tonight, after supper, I can start cutting out the dresses, though, and we'll work on them in the evenings and any time we have a little extra time during the day. Do you want me to make your Sunday dresses first?"

Both girls nodded. "I want mine done for church on Sunday!" Victoria said excitedly.

"I'll do my best. That's cutting it close, but I made a lot of dresses for the orphans from whatever scrap fabric was donated, and I got to be pretty quick about it." Caroline was thrilled that Victoria seemed to be warming up to her, though she had a feeling it wouldn't last.

"I'll work as hard as it takes to get mine done on time," Victoria said.

"I'll help with Victoria's. We'll start mine after," Amy offered. "She needs hers more than I need mine."

Caroline hated to admit it, but Amy was right. Victoria's dresses were about to pop at the seams. "Do you girls know how to make any meals on your own?" she asked.

Victoria and Amy exchanged a look, both of them shaking their heads. "No, ma'am," Amy answered for both of them.

"All right. I was thinking I could start cutting out the first dress while the two of you fixed supper, but that won't work. We'll do it after supper."

Victoria frowned. "If you could tell us what to do, maybe we could make it right."

"Do you want to try?" Caroline asked. She was surprised that Victoria was volunteering to do anything. She must really want that dress done by Sunday.

Amy nodded. "I'll try. You've taught us a lot, and the bread is already made."

"All right. I'll try to direct you on what to do while I cut out the first dress." Caroline rubbed her hands together, ready to get started. "We do have to plant the garden first thing, or I would do it. It's already getting late in the spring, and from what I've read, the crops need to be harvested before the full heat of the summer."

"We know how to plant," Amy said. "Why don't we start the planting while you work on the dress?"

"Really? You girls have helped plant a kitchen garden before?" When they both nodded, Caroline smiled. "Then that's how we'll start. I'll get to work right away."

So while the girls put on their oldest clothes and planted seeds where their father had someone plow a small portion of land for their garden, Caroline cut out Victoria's church dress.

As soon as they'd had supper, the girls rushed to do the dishes, so they could help with the sewing. Andrew frowned at Caroline. "Why are you in such a hurry to sew this?" He was feeling a little bit neglected with all three of the women in his house focused on only the dress.

"Victoria would like to have it for church on Sunday." Caroline smiled at Andrew. "The girls planted the entire garden by themselves, and they made most of supper with only a little help."

"Really?" he asked, surprised.

"Really. Victoria is very excited, and she's asking lots of questions. I'm going to give her two small pieces to sew together when they finish the dishes."

He was surprised when both girls came in ready to help. There was so much excitement in the house over the new dresses, he was surprised it was the same place. Victoria seemed to have forgotten her hatred of Caroline as they worked together, and Amy was happily working on her sister's dress and not asking for one of her own.

He whittled while his women-folk sewed and talked about what they'd planted that day. The girls were both talking about the home-grown vegetables they'd have that fall, and he was a little startled at their enthusiasm.

After a while, Caroline laughed. "Girls, we've talked of our day and nothing else all evening. How was your day, Andrew?"

He shrugged. "Mostly good. The cows are still dropping calves at an alarming rate. We did get the one calf to be adopted by another cow, but now we have another whose mother rejected him. There were twins, and she wanted nothing to do with the smaller one, which really isn't uncommon."

"We're still open for bottle feeding if that's what we need to do," Caroline said, and Amy nodded emphatically. "It would be hard to finish our dress on time, but we'd make it work."

"I think we're getting it taken care of." He rubbed the back of his neck. "I did see that the barn cat had kittens today."

"Tom?" Amy asked. "I thought Tom was a boy!"

"We all did. Tammy had kittens."

"Can we have one for the house?" Victoria asked. "I've always wanted a kitten."

Andrew almost said no immediately, but he paused. "Cats don't make you sneeze, do they?" he asked Caroline.

Caroline shook her head. "No, they never have."

"How would you feel about an inside cat, then? We tend to get mice in the house sometimes, and the cat would take care of it. We have barn cats, but they don't take care of the ones in the house. We never could have a house cat because Marie got sick when there were cats around, but if you don't . . ."

Caroline smiled and nodded. "I wouldn't mind at all, but it would have to be Victoria's responsibility if it was her cat. She'd need to do all the caretaking."

"I will! Oh, I promise I will!" Victoria dropped her sewing. "I want to go see them right now!"

"I don't think so," Andrew said. "Tomorrow is soon enough. They can't be taken from their mother for six weeks anyway."

Victoria reluctantly picked her sewing back up. "But I can choose which one I want tomorrow?"

"Yes, you can choose the one you want tomorrow." Andrew's eyes met Caroline's, and she smiled. The girl seemed to finally be warming up to having her around.

After the girls were in bed that night, Caroline kept working on the dress, wanting to have as much done before morning as she possibly could. She hated that Victoria had been running around in ill-fitting dresses for who knew how long.

Finally, just before ten, Andrew frowned at her. "Are you going to work on that all night, or are you going to go to bed with your husband?"

Caroline tilted her head to one side, looking at him. "So my choices are staying down here and working, or going to bed with you and playing . . . that's a hard choice."

He laughed, taking the sewing from her hands. "I promise it will still be here in the morning when you're ready to sew some more."

"You sure? What if one of the girls sneaks down and takes it up to her room to sew? Or what if an elf comes and finishes it while I sleep?"

"An elf?" Andrew was certain the woman had lost her mind.

"Have you never read the story of the shoemaker and the elves? It was always one of my favorites when I was a girl."

"You'll have to tell it to me after . . ."

"After?"

"Sure, your story can be the lullaby that puts me right to sleep." He took her hand and started pulling her toward the stairs. "I've waited all day for this, and you just sit there sewing like you don't know your husband is going slightly crazy with his need to love you."

She shook her head, laughing. "What did you do before I came?"

"I went to bed sad every single night," he told her with a wink.

THE GIRLS HAD A HARD time sitting through their lessons the following morning, because they so desperately wanted to work on the dress. Caroline made the dough for their bread, and while it rose, she sat at the table with them and sewed. She had a nice crocheted collar she'd made on the train on the way there that she planned to put on the dress, though she didn't tell Victoria that. She wanted her to be surprised.

The girls planted the flowers in the afternoon, and as soon as they were done, they washed up and helped with the sewing. Caroline had put on a huge pot of soup after lunch so that they wouldn't have to worry about cooking for supper.

When Andrew walked into the house that evening, he heard laughter coming from the parlor, and three voices were heard. He followed his ears and stood at the doorway listening as Caroline told a story about identical twins who had lived in the orphanage who had kept changing places.

As soon as the story was over, he cleared his throat. "I thought Victoria might want to look at the kittens before supper."

Victoria set her sewing down and jumped to her feet. "Oh, yes!" She hurried after her father out of the house.

Amy looked at Caroline with a big smile. "She likes you. She doesn't want to like you, but she just can't help it."

Caroline laughed. "I'm sure we'll have more troubles before it's all done, but I'm glad she likes me for now. It makes things a little easier for me."

"For all of us," Amy said. "Tomorrow's the day Amanda Anderson comes over, isn't it?"

"I'd all but forgotten! We'll have to make some cookies in the morning to serve with our tea. Will you girls join us?"

Amy shook her head. "Oh, no. Mom never let us sit with her and Mrs. Anderson. We'll keep working on the dress or do something else. Anything else."

"You don't like Amanda?"

Amy shrugged. "Mom seemed to, so we're polite to her."

"All right. I'll reserve judgment until I've gotten to know her, then."

"I like that about you."

"What?" Caroline asked. Amy was so sweet and always saying what she liked about Caroline. It was nice.

"That you don't take other people's word for things and you figure it out on your own." Amy shrugged. "Most people form their opinions before they give a person a chance."

The door opened, then, and Victoria came in clutching a tiny little gray ball of fur to her chest. "This is the one I want. We're going to name her Patch, because she has one white eye." She walked to her sister with the kitten. "Do you want to hold her?"

Amy reached out and held the kitten just under her chin. "She's so soft!"

Caroline smiled, happy to see the girls with a pet. She thought every child should have a pet at least once. She'd had a little bunny rabbit when she was a girl. "I'm glad you found one you like."

Victoria looked at Caroline. "Thank you for letting me have her."

"You're very welcome."

Andrew took the kitten from Amy. "I think this little one needs to get back to her mama now. Tom—I mean Tammy—did not look happy with us for taking her away."

Victoria washed her hands and set the table without being asked. "I'm starving. This soup smells delicious."

Caroline wasn't sure what to do with the compliment, so she just said, "I hope it tastes as good as it smells."

By the time Andrew was back, the table was set and they were ready to eat. "We made soup today to make it easier for us to get the sewing done. I hope that's all right." Caroline wasn't sure what kind of meals Andrew expected, but she would do her best to keep him and his daughters fed and happy.

"Sounds good. As long as there's lots of chunks in it, so it fills me up."

"There are plenty of chunks." Caroline used a ladle to put soup into a bowl and was surprised to see Victoria there to carry it to the table. Amy was pouring milk for everyone. She felt as if something was going horribly wrong with the way Victoria was acting, but she wasn't about to look a gift horse in the mouth.

After the prayer, they all began eating, and Victoria praised the soup. "This is so good. I'm glad you showed us how to make it."

"I'm happy to teach you anything you want to learn, Victoria. And I'll probably teach you some things you have no desire to learn, just because I feel like you should know them."

Amy hid her grin behind her soup spoon.

Once they finished eating, the girls once again went straight to the dishes, while Caroline sat down and sewed more. "We had a sewing machine at home, and sometimes I would take some of the sewing from the orphanage home with me and get it done faster to surprise the children. I wish I had somewhere to sneak this so that I could have it finished quickly."

"It looks like it's close to being done," Andrew said.

"Mostly. I need to add the buttons and buttonholes. And there's still some hemming that needs to be done." Caroline lowered her voice. "And I have a collar that I crocheted on the train on the way here I'm going to add. It will make the dress look a lot fancier and more grown up."

"I don't want my daughters growing up too quickly now . . ."

She grinned. "Of course, you don't. But you don't really have a choice."

"How's the schoolwork coming along?"

"They don't like it much, but they're doing it. Amy is fussing over the arithmetic, but she's understanding it." Caroline shrugged. "Do you agree with me that the girls need to be able to do basic arithmetic?"

"Absolutely. I think they should learn whatever you're willing to teach them." He picked up his block of wood and carving knife, turning the wood over in his hand.

"What are you looking for?" she asked.

"I'm trying to figure out what the wood wants to be. There's an animal in there just begging to come out, but I'm not sure what yet."

Caroline smiled and leaned toward him, whispering. "Maybe a little gray kitten for a girl who needs to feel loved."

He grinned and nodded. "I have some paint. I can make that happen." He set to work on it, his fingers expertly shaving off pieces of the wood. "I don't know why it never occurred to me that a girl might want one of the animals I make. I thought they were just for boys."

"Well, I for one loved the bunny you gave me. I think the girls would feel very special to get one of the animals you're always working on."

"Really?"

"Really. Just like they're so excited about this dress. And Amy was very happy to learn to make butter. I think they are happy with anything that we spend time on. With them or for them. They're good kids, and I know they've caused some problems, but I think they just really wanted more of your attention than you knew how to give them."

He frowned. "I did kind of expect the housekeepers to take care of them and teach them anything they needed to know."

Caroline shook her head. "They didn't teach them. Amy told me they preferred it if the girls were out of the way."

"I really did the best I could for them." He shook his head. "I thank God for the day the agency told me they'd send no more housekeepers and I realized I'd have to send for a wife."

She frowned at him. "You didn't *want* a wife? You just wanted another housekeeper?"

"I needed someone to help me, and I didn't know what else to do. I'm glad you came."

She didn't know how to respond to that. He'd wanted a housekeeper and not a bride, and she'd been dreaming about falling in love and happily ever after. What was wrong with her?

Chapter Eight

THE GIRLS MADE THEMSELVES scarce when it was time for Amanda to arrive the following afternoon. Caroline had made sugar cookies and tea, and she'd set everything out nicely.

When Amanda arrived, Caroline watched her closely, trying to understand what it was about her that Amy didn't like. It didn't take long. "Oh, I see you are using Marie's prized tea set. She never let anyone touch it. It was just for looks."

Caroline couldn't help but wonder if the other woman thought she shouldn't use the tea set, but she was going to. She had another one that was just as nice in her hope chest she'd brought with her, so if something broke, she'd just replace it with her own. Possessions didn't matter. If you couldn't use something, what was the purpose of having it?

"Well, I think it looks just lovely on the table with tea and cookies. Don't you?" Caroline finally asked. She sat down at the table and poured tea for both of them. "How long have you lived in this area?"

Amanda sat down, seeming a little annoyed that she hadn't gotten a bigger reaction from Caroline. "I've been here my whole life. Marie and I were neighbors growing up, and we were best friends from the time we were little girls."

"Oh, how wonderful. So you've known the girls since they were tiny."

"Yes. They're hellions, but I have always tolerated that. Marie and Andrew were terrible parents, letting the girls run amok." Amanda shook her head. "She never took advice from any of us who had well-behaved children either."

Run amok. It had always been a favorite phrase of Caroline's. She wanted to run amok and hug the girls to her. This woman was *not* going to be a friend of hers; that was for certain. "The girls were a little difficult to get to know at first, but I find them to be very sweet." It was a bit of a stretch to call both girls sweet, but she wasn't going to let this woman insult her new daughters.

"Oh, please. I know Victoria, and Amy is following right along in her footsteps. Did you know that Victoria screamed at Marie right before she died? She was yelling at her for thinking the baby was more important than her daughters." Amanda shook her head. "Horrible girl."

"I'm sure she regrets it now." The other woman's story actually helped Caroline understand Victoria better. She probably felt a great deal of guilt for the way she'd treated her mother right before her death. "I can't imagine how horrible I would feel if I'd done that right before my mother died. I don't know that I could live with myself."

"You sound like you actually feel bad for the brat!" Amanda took a bite of her cookie. "You put too much sugar in these. Perhaps if you added a little less, they'd be palatable."

Caroline took a deep breath and smiled. "I'm sorry they're not to your liking." Caroline put them all onto her own plate. "There, now you won't feel compelled to eat any more of them."

Amanda's eyes narrowed. "I think you've been spending too much time with the girls. Their manners are rubbing off on you."

"Perhaps their actions were learned from their mother's ill-mannered friend." Caroline stood. "I'm sorry that you don't think I should be using these dishes, defending my new daughters, or baking with as much sugar as I do. If ever I do start living up to your expectations, let me know, and you can come back." She walked to the door and opened it. "Good day."

Amanda's jaw dropped as she headed for the door. "I can't believe how rude you are!"

"I was always taught to treat others the way I want to be treated. Obviously, you want to be treated rudely, because you've been nothing but rude to me from the moment you stepped into my house. Good day." Caroline waited until Amanda was outside before she shut the door. She didn't wait to see the other woman to her wagon as she usually would have. She wanted nothing more to do with her.

As soon as the door shut, both girls came from the stairs. Victoria stood for a moment, just looking at her, but Amy flew into her arms. "Thank you!"

Caroline frowned at Amy. "For what?" She stroked the girl's back, happy to be embraced.

"For defending us."

BY SUNDAY MORNING, Victoria's dress was finished. Caroline woke up early to put the collar on it so it would be perfect. She took it into Victoria's room when she woke her for church, laying it over the foot of the bed. "Time to wake up. Your dress is ready." She closed the door behind her and went on to wake Amy. "Breakfast is ready."

When they'd all gathered for breakfast, Victoria was in her new dress, and she looked like the young lady she was instead of the little girl the other dresses had made her look like.

"How do you like it?" Caroline asked.

Victoria gave a little spin. "It's perfect. I feel like a fairytale princess." Her whole face was lit up with excitement at wearing the new dress.

"Too bad the elves couldn't finish it," Andrew mumbled as he sat down with his breakfast. He was a little annoyed at all the time his new wife had put into making a dress for his unappreciative daughter.

Caroline shook her head at him. "I'm so glad you like it."

"I can't wait until the other girls see it today!" Victoria fiddled with the collar. "I didn't see this before. Where did it come from?"

"I made it on the train on the way here. I knew we'd use it for something."

"It's beautiful. Thank you, Caroline."

"You're very welcome." Caroline waved to the table. "Sit and eat. We don't want to be late for church. I let you both sleep later than usual this morning." She didn't add they'd slept later because she had been playing in bed with their father, knowing that was something neither of them ever needed to know.

Amy kept looking at Victoria and grinning. "You look beautiful, 'Toria," she finally said.

"Thank you," Victoria said with a smile. "We'll start on your dress next."

"Actually, I think we should do another of yours first, Victoria, if that's all right with Amy. Hers still fit, but yours are busting at the seams."

Victoria nodded. "If Amy doesn't mind."

Amy shrugged. "I'm getting three new dresses. I have nothing to complain about."

After breakfast, the girls both put on their new aprons they'd made that week and did the dishes together while Caroline hurried upstairs and put on one of her Sunday dresses. She had come from a relatively wealthy family, and she had always had six or seven Sunday dresses to choose from.

When Andrew stepped up behind her and wrapped his arms around her, she leaned back against him. "You never told me how your visit with Amanda went. That *was* this week, wasn't it?"

She groaned, turning in his arms. "I don't think you want to know."

"That bad, huh? Marie used to say she'd come in and complain about everything. If she was using an old tea set, she should use the new one. If she used the new one, she should be more careful not to break her nice things. She complained about the girls constantly. Marie didn't know how to get her to stay away."

Caroline smiled. "I think I figured it out. I opened the door and told her to go. I have a feeling she won't be back."

"Did you really?"

She nodded. "She was just like you said. She complained about your parenting. She complained about the girls. She complained about how much sugar I put in my sugar cookies. If I'd had to listen to her for another minute, I think I would have started throwing the nice tea cups that I shouldn't have been using."

He laughed. "Did she tell you that? I'm not at all surprised. I should have warned you, but I was hoping it wouldn't be as bad for you as it was for Marie. I guess I was wrong."

She sighed. "At least she can't complain about how Victoria's dressed today. I'm sure she'll talk about me, because she's that kind of woman, but I just don't care. I have everything I need right here under this roof. A good man, two daughters who sometimes like me a little bit, and a home to live in. What more could a mail-order bride ask for?" *Maybe a man who had actually wanted a bride and not a housekeeper.*

"There's a small diner in town that's mainly for people coming to pick up train passengers. I was thinking maybe we could have lunch there after church, so you don't need to cook."

"I'd better not. What would people think? I'm sure Marie cooked every single meal as she went about her perfect life." A little bit of bitterness crept into her voice and even surprised Caroline. It was hard to compete with a dead woman.

Andrew shook his head emphatically. "We went there all the time. Marie hated to cook. She would beg me to take her out to eat every chance we had."

"Really? That truly is the first negative thing I've heard about her—other than what Amanda said, and I didn't listen to that crazy woman."

He smiled. "She was far from perfect, but she was my first love and the mother of my children. We had a good marriage, and I won't speak ill about her."

"The girls don't either. It seems that Victoria practically worships her."

"She didn't when she was alive. Just keep that in mind when she's telling you how wonderful her mother was." Andrew sighed. "We need to get to church. I'm going to take you out to lunch, and then we're going for another walk. I liked our walk last Sunday. Did you?"

She nodded. "I loved it. It made me feel very courted."

"I'll try to keep courting you, even though I've had you in my bed for a week now." Andrew wiggled his eyebrows at her. "I plan on having you in my bed tonight, too."

She shook her head. "You are *insatiable,* Mr. Dawson."

When they got to church, all of the other girls crowded around Victoria, and they were obviously admiring her dress. As Caroline watched, she smiled, pleased the girl was getting some positive attention.

She saw Amanda look at her and wrinkle her nose, immediately turning to another woman and saying something that just felt like it was negative to Caroline from across the room. Caroline walked over to the two women. "I saw you admiring Victoria's dress. We worked all week on it. Isn't it beautiful?"

The two women exchanged a look. "It is beautiful," the woman Caroline hadn't met yet said. "I'm Dorothy Grappling."

"Caroline Dawson. Victoria was so excited there was finally someone to sew for her. I'm surprised none of her mother's *dear friends* stepped up to help out when the girls were obviously outgrowing everything they had. I'm happy they didn't, though, because it gives me something to do. I do hate to be idle."

Amanda's eyes widened. "Are you saying I did something wrong by not sewing for the girls? There were always housekeepers there that could have done it."

"Not with the love a mother or a mother's best friend would have sewn with." Caroline smiled. "It was so nice to meet you, Dorothy. I hope we'll be friends." She walked to the pew where she'd sat with her family the week before and settled down into it. She knew if she stayed close to Amanda for any period of time, she might just have to snatch the woman baldheaded.

Andrew sat down next to her. "The sermon today is on kindness. The pastor pulls this one out at least once a year. I think it's mostly aimed toward one person in the congregation."

Caroline grinned. "I shouldn't be happy about that, but it does make me smile. The woman needs to be put in her place."

The girls came over and sat with them, then. "Did you get any compliments on your dress, Victoria?" Caroline asked.

"Yes, everyone loves it. They said the collar is beautiful, and they want some just like it. Would you teach me to make them? They'd be nice Christmas gifts for my friends." Victoria seemed embarrassed to ask.

"I would love to teach you." Caroline looked at Amy. "Want to learn something new?"

"Always!" Amy said with a smile, hugging Caroline's arm. "I'm glad you came to marry Dad."

Caroline floated on air through the whole service because of that one phrase from Amy. The sermon was on kindness, and everyone seemed to be looking at Amanda, which made Caroline feel even better. She hadn't been singled out for the other woman to be rude to. It was just who she was. When Caroline realized that, she started to feel sorry for her. The woman would truly never have a real friend because she didn't know how to treat people. Hopefully someday, she would change, but Caroline did not need to be the person to teach her how. She had her hands full with her girls.

The diner was packed after church, and they found a table in the corner. The food was wonderful, and Caroline was halfway through her meal when the waitress came back to refill their water glasses. "How's everything?"

"It's wonderful," Caroline said softly.

"The food isn't as good as our Caroline's," Victoria said, not looking up from her food. She was obviously embarrassed to give the compliment.

Caroline's eyes met Andrew's, and he smiled, nodding. He knew she was finally getting through to his daughter, and he was happy about it.

"Tomorrow we're going to start one of Victoria's everyday dresses, and then I think we need to make Amy's church dress." Caroline smiled at the younger girl. "I want you to get the same compliments Victoria got."

"Me too," Victoria said softly. "I'll help. I want Amy to feel as good about how she looks as I did today."

"We're going for another walk today. Are you girls coming?"

Amy nodded emphatically. "I am!"

Victoria smiled. "I'd like to come, too. I promise I'll act better than I did last time."

"That would be nice," Andrew said, shaking his head at her. "You do look awfully beautiful in your new dress. Just like your mother."

Victoria sat up straighter at his words, obviously feeling that looking like her mother was a compliment.

While they walked, both girls told stories about different things that had happened on the ranch. They went a different way, and Andrew showed Caroline the homestead where they'd originally lived on the land. "It was only two rooms and so small."

Caroline poked her head into the empty house and smiled. "I can't imagine all of you living there."

"It was tight," Andrew said. "We were all happy once I got the new house built. I should have done it sooner, but I was determined to do it without taking out a loan, so I waited until I had everything I needed to buy the supplies for the house I wanted to build. Marie died just a few months after we moved in. I've always regretted not getting a loan so she could live more comfortably for longer."

Victoria stood in the middle of the small room, looking around her. "I can almost hear Mom calling me to come and do my schoolwork. She always made us sit all day every day doing school while she did the housework. We never really got to learn anything from her except school."

"Do you regret that?" Caroline asked.

Victoria nodded. "I regret a lot of things. But we'll never get our mom back."

Caroline frowned, but she said nothing else. It seemed like a moment for the people who had known Marie to grieve her, and she had never met the woman, though she loved her family with everything inside her.

She stepped out of the little house and walked a few feet away, feeling at a loss. She was taking the place of a woman who had died, but her husband had never wanted anything but a housekeeper. He'd felt forced to get a mail-order bride, but there she was, and she wasn't going anywhere. The love she'd dreamed of wasn't there . . . at least not on his side.

The girls she'd dreamed would take one look at her and think of her as a mother still seemed a little unsure about her. Nothing was going as she'd planned. The thought of even reading one of her romance novels wasn't pleasant, because real life was different than the happily ever afters she'd always dreamed of.

When the family joined her after their moment in the little house, they continued walking, but Caroline found she'd lost a great deal of her enjoyment. She wanted love. She'd thought a mail-order bride arrangement would be enough and they would immediately feel a great deal of love for each other, but he was still in love with his dead wife.

She was going to have to get over the fact that she wanted things to be so different. Instead, she was going to have to be the wife and mother everyone needed her to be, and hopefully, one day in the not too distant future, one of them would realize that she was lovable, and she would be a true part of their family. Not just a housekeeper who was trying to parent and be a wife. Until then, she would mourn for the dreams of what could have been, but she could never let it show.

Chapter Nine

THE NEXT WEEK WAS A whirl of activity as they worked on the garden and kept sewing. Caroline finished the first of Victoria's everyday dresses on Wednesday morning, and the girl held the dress in front of her as soon as she woke up. "I didn't know you were this far along!"

"I've been working on it after you go to bed at night and before you wake up in the mornings. I knew you needed something that fit you."

Victoria squealed. "I'm going to go upstairs and change right now!" Victoria ran up the stairs, passing Amy on the way.

Amy was still rubbing her eyes when she got to the kitchen. "What's 'Toria so excited about?"

"I finished her dress, so now we can start on yours today."

"Really?" Amy's face lit up, though it looked awfully pale to Caroline. "I didn't think we were anywhere close to working on one of mine."

"Well, we are. Do you want me to do your Sunday dress first or one of your everyday dresses?"

"Sunday dress, please. And I want a collar like 'Toria's, if you don't mind."

Caroline nodded. "I'll cut your dress out this morning, and I'll show you girls how to crochet the collars this afternoon." She knew she'd probably have to crochet this first collar, but that was fine. The girls would be learning something new. One of her favorite things in the whole world was learning, and she wanted to instill that in her new daughters.

Amy took her breakfast from Caroline, yawning as she sat down. "I feel like I barely slept last night."

Caroline frowned at her. "Are you sick?"

Amy shrugged. "I don't think so. Maybe."

After a moment, Caroline walked to Amy and put the back of her hand against her forehead. "You're burning up! You need to get back to bed."

"But I'm hungry."

"Eat then go back to bed. No helping around the house today. Do you feel badly?"

Amy thought for a moment. "My chest feels heavy. Like something is sitting on it."

Caroline's eyes met Andrew's. "Is there a doctor close?"

"Is she that bad? I'm sure it's just a cold."

"I don't think so. Her fever is high."

"I'll ride to town and see if I can get Dr. Duncan to drive out and check on her." Andrew ate his last bite of food and got to his feet. "I'll be back as soon as I can." He was certain Caroline was worried for nothing, but he'd get the doctor to appease her. He didn't want to risk anything happening to his daughter.

After breakfast, Amy headed back up to bed, and Victoria helped with the dishes. "Is Amy really that sick?" Victoria asked, looking toward the stairs.

"I don't know, but she was very hot, and she wasn't feeling well. My mother died of influenza, and I probably worry more about sickness than I should. I would just rather be safe."

Victoria frowned. "How old were you when your mother died?"

Caroline thought she'd talked to Victoria about it, but it was in her early days at the ranch when Victoria was ignoring everything she said. "I was thirteen. My father remarried six months later, because he thought a girl my age needed a mother. I hated my stepmother with everything inside me."

"You really did?"

"I really did. Now, she's one of my favorite people. I've already sent her three letters since I got here."

"So you don't hate her anymore?" Victoria asked.

"How can I hate the woman who did so much for me? She is the one who threw my coming out party. All of my friends were there in ball gowns, and I was the star of the evening. She even made my dress, while all of my friends' mothers hired someone to make theirs. She told me that it was a labor of love." Caroline shook her head. "From the day she married my father, she showed me only love and acceptance."

Victoria seemed to want to say something, but Andrew came in then with Dr. Duncan.

Caroline dried her hands on her apron as she rushed toward the man. "Thank you so much for coming. I may be panicking over nothing, but it looks to me as if she has influenza."

The doctor looked at her for a moment. "And who have you lost to influenza?"

"My mother." She knew that he thought she was panicking unnecessarily, and she didn't care. As long as Amy was all right, nothing else mattered.

"I'll check on her. Please come with me."

Caroline hurried up the stairs, showing the doctor the way. Amy's door was open, and she walked inside, sitting on the side of Amy's bed. "Dr. Duncan came to see how you were doing."

Amy struggled to sit up. "I'm all right. I just have this tightness right here." She pointed to the center of her chest.

The doctor took out his stethoscope and listened to her before smiling and nodding. "I'm going to talk with your mother, and she'll be right back."

Caroline stepped out into the hallway with the doctor, closing the door behind her. "Is she all right?"

"I think she will be with proper care. You did the right thing in sending for me. It looks like influenza. You'll need to give her water and chicken broth. As much as she'll drink. And I want her to stay in bed. You should be the one to take care of her and only you. Wash your hands every time you leave her room to keep the disease from spreading. Make sure she covers her mouth when she coughs. Send for me if she gets any worse."

She nodded, fear filling her eyes. "She's young and strong."

"Yes, she is. Most people do not die from influenza."

"I'll do my best to care for her, but I'd appreciate it if you'd stop by when you have time."

The doctor nodded. "I'll make sure I come by on Friday morning. Do not take her to church on Sunday by any means."

"Of course not. I'll do my best to take care of her."

Dr. Duncan headed down the stairs, and Caroline opened Amy's door, going into her room and smiling down at the girl. "Well, I was right. You have influenza. Lucky for you, I've taken care of people with it before. You're going to be fine." Caroline said a silent prayer that she wasn't lying to Amy. She had taken care of several orphans with influenza since her mother's death, and all had been fine, so she felt she could be positive.

Amy nodded. "I'm so sleepy."

"You sleep. I'm going to go put on a pot of chicken soup, and I'll bring you some later." Caroline smiled down at the girl. "I'll work on your collar today, and we'll have it ready to go on your dress as soon as it's made."

"You'll show me soon?"

"As soon as you're better, I'll show you just how to do it."

Amy's eyes drifted closed, and Caroline hurried out of the room and down the stairs. She started the pot of chicken soup and got a glass of water to carry up the stairs to Amy. Victoria had tears in her eyes. "I'll take it up to her."

"Right now, the doctor wants me to be the only one taking care of her. I'll be back in a minute, and we'll start working on her dress."

Victoria nodded. "Maybe we can have it ready for her by the time she's feeling better."

Caroline smiled and nodded. "Let's get to work on it as soon as we have the morning chores finished. If we work together, we can get most of it done quickly."

"I would really like to try to do that." Victoria seemed very excited at the idea. "Can I try to make her collar?"

"Absolutely. If you run into trouble with it, let me know, but I'll cut out the dress." Caroline was pleased to see Victoria doing something for someone else. She'd been kind since they'd started making dresses for her, but Caroline had expected it to stop as soon as it was time to turn their attention to Amy. "Let's get the kitchen cleaned, and we'll get the dress started."

An hour later, Victoria was sitting at the table, her brow furrowed as she worked on crocheting a collar while Caroline carefully cut out the pieces of Amy's dress.

As soon as the dress was cut out, Caroline fixed a bowl of the soup, mainly just the broth, and carried it up the stairs for Amy. "The doctor wants you to eat as much of this as you can." She saw that the girl's water glass was still full from earlier. "And you have to try to drink water."

Amy nodded, her eyes puffy. "I'll try." She struggled into a sitting position.

"Do you want me to stay with you?"

"No, I just want to sleep."

"Eat first, then." Caroline hurried from the room and down the stairs. She wanted to stay with Amy, but at the same time, she wanted to finish her dress.

When it was time for her to start sewing, she and Victoria moved into the parlor. "Do you miss your family?" Victoria asked, surprising Caroline.

"I do. Some. But I'm happy to have another family. I know this is where I belong. With you and Amy and your dad. I love it here." *I feel useful for the first time in my life. I feel needed.*

"I don't hate you anymore," Victoria said, her eyes still on her work.

"I'm glad." From Victoria, that was like a declaration of intense love.

By lunchtime, most of the dress had been basted together, and Caroline was ready to actually start sewing. Amy's dress would be simpler than Victoria's, so the sewing was going much faster.

Just as the two of them were sitting down to lunch together, Andrew came into the room, a wooden crate in his arms. He put it down on the floor and left for a moment, leaving Caroline and Victoria looking at the object, wondering what on earth it could be.

When he came back in with a hammer a moment later, he opened the box and took out a sewing machine on a stand. Caroline covered her mouth with one hand. She knew how pricey sewing machines were, and she couldn't believe he'd parted with that much money to purchase it for her.

"Are you sure?" Caroline asked as she got to her feet to touch the precious object.

He nodded. "I ordered it a week ago. I want you to be able to sew as quickly as you can." He stepped back and rubbed the back of his neck, a little embarrassed at how excited she was about the gift.

Caroline didn't think about what she was doing, but she rushed to him and threw her arms around his neck, kissing him. "Thank you!"

"You're very welcome. Put it to good use. How's Amy?"

Caroline frowned. "She's not doing great, but she's holding her own. I'm trying to get her to eat and drink as much as she can, and Victoria and I are hurrying to finish her dress before she's well."

Andrew smiled. "Thank you for thinking of her that way."

"She's mine now, too."

"I'm getting back to work." He hurried from the house, obviously embarrassed about something.

Caroline returned to the table and sat down with Victoria. "Can you believe we have a sewing machine? Sewing is going to be so much easier now!"

Victoria had a perplexed look on her face. "I want to hate you for kissing my dad, when only my mom is supposed to do it. But my mom died."

"I know how you feel. I was exactly the same when Francis, my stepmother, moved in with us. It was strange knowing that my father was married to someone other than my mother." Caroline frowned. "I'm sorry if that bothered you."

"I think it bothers me more that it *didn't* bother me, if that makes sense." Victoria shrugged, trying to figure out what to say. "I want to always be loyal to my mother and think you're a horrible person for kissing my dad, but it's hard to feel that way when you're so kind to me and Amy."

"I'll always be kind to both of you. I care about you."

"I know. I can tell. You're not pretending like the housekeepers did. It's real."

"The housekeepers pretended?"

Victoria nodded. "I think some of them just took the job because they wanted to get married, and they thought that being a housekeeper to a widower with two girls was going to be a way to marry him. It never worked out, though."

"Because of the tricks you and Amy played?" Caroline was thrilled Victoria was opening up to her, and she asked more and more questions to get to the bottom of what the girl was feeling.

"Partially. None of them wanted to be here, though. None of them enjoyed cooking and cleaning like you do." Victoria tilted her head to one side, studying her stepmother. "You really do like it, don't you? It's not an act."

"No, it's not an act at all. I've always enjoyed cooking, cleaning, and being around children. Sewing and crocheting are fun to me. I know I should not enjoy work quite as much as I do, but I don't care. I do enjoy it, and I'm not going to hide it because it's not quite what others expect of me."

"Amy has always liked those things, too. I was more like my mom. We both hated to clean. Mom hated cooking, too. She would wait until right before Dad came home and do as much as she could really quick so it looked like she'd been working all day. But she never had been."

Caroline was surprised. She wasn't sure if Victoria was exactly criticizing her mother, but these weren't the glowing words that normally came from her mouth. "Did that bother you?"

Victoria shrugged. "Not really. I thought everyone was that way until you came here."

"Well, I guess I'm the odd one, but that's all right." Caroline walked to the sink with both of their empty bowls to wash them. "Would you mind washing our dishes so I can check on your sister?"

Victoria immediately walked over to do as she was asked. Caroline still wondered when the girl would return to how she'd been before, but she was thrilled with her obedient attitude now.

Climbing the stairs, she wondered how their patient was doing, hoping that Amy's fever would have broken and she was feeling better when she got up there.

Instead, Amy was lying on her back sound asleep. Only about half of the soup was gone, but the glass was empty. Caroline was pleased with the progress but still worried about the girl. She put the back of her hand on her forehead and felt that her fever seemed a little lower but not enough lower to celebrate.

She took the soup bowl downstairs and refilled the water, carrying it back up. Amy slept through the whole thing. Caroline was worried but also glad she was sleeping so much. She just hoped it was a healing sleep.

When she got back downstairs, the dishes were all washed, and Victoria was once again sitting at the table with her crocheting. "Are you going to use the sewing machine now?"

Caroline nodded. "I'm to the point in this dress where the sewing machine will be very useful. I feel a little bad that your father paid that much for the machine, but I'm glad to have it."

"Oh, Dad doesn't mind spending money." Victoria didn't look up as she worked on the collar. "I think I made a knot. Can you help?"

Caroline hurried over and worked the knot out before going back to the machine and putting her feet on the treadle. She was excited to get this dress done quickly now. The machine was just like her stepmother's, so she knew exactly how to use it.

She had the dress mostly done when she set it aside two hours later to go up and check on Amy. The girl was awake this time, and her water glass was empty. "Would you like some more broth? Or do you just want to keep drinking water?"

"I'm not hungry. Just more water, please."

"I'll bring you up a book as well," Caroline said, taking the water glass with her. She wondered if *Jane Eyre* was too advanced for Amy and decided it was. She'd take her *Little Women* instead. She was sure Amy would love the adventures of Meg, Jo, Beth, and Amy March.

When she arrived back upstairs with the book and the water, Amy took the book and looked at it. "I think you'll really like this book. It's about four young women who live in Boston around the time of the Civil War," Caroline told her.

"I'll read it." Amy looked sleepy. "I think I'm going to sleep some more now, though."

"You do that. Sleeping is the best thing for you. If you get bored and want to read, the book is here."

"Thank you." Amy turned onto her side and went straight back to sleep.

Caroline tiptoed out of the room and returned to her sewing machine. "If we have the soup I made for supper, we can probably finish this dress before we eat."

Victoria frowned. "The collar won't be done."

"That's all right. Amy isn't going to be up and around for a couple of days yet. I can work on the collar if you'd like."

"No, I want to do it. I want Amy to know that I helped because I love her."

Caroline smiled. "That's good of you." She turned back to the machine and continued sewing, thrilled that everything was going so quickly. Amy didn't seem to be nearly as sick as her mother had been either. She felt strongly that the girl was going to be all right.

When Andrew came in a few hours later, she held up the finished dress—sans the collar—and showed him how well it had turned out. "I think I'll work on an everyday dress for her tomorrow. Amy is going to have a new wardrobe when she feels better."

He smiled. "How's she doing?"

Caroline shrugged. "She's drinking lots of water, and she had half a bowl of broth earlier, but she's been sleeping most of the day."

"What did the doctor say about that?"

"Dr. Duncan wants her to sleep, drink lots of fluids, and sleep some more. Sleep is healing for her."

He nodded. "I should go up and see her."

"That's fine, but don't go into the room. The doctor wants only me to be around her, and I have to wash my hands when I leave. He's hoping that will keep the influenza from spreading."

"All right. If she wants something, I'll let you know." He headed up the stairs, very worried about his younger daughter. He'd already lost his wife and a son. He didn't think he could lose another child and keep his sanity. He opened her door and stood quietly, watching her sleep for a moment. She looked so pale to him. Closing the door, he went back downstairs, lost in thought. He had thought Amy looked fine that morning and Caroline was overreacting. He didn't think so anymore.

He was quiet through supper and wasn't surprised that the others seemed quiet and worried as well. It was late in the year for influenza, but apparently it was still going around town.

After supper, Caroline took Amy some soup and woke her, telling her she needed to eat to keep up her strength. "I need you to eat as much as you can." She sat down on the edge of the girl's bed. "How are you feeling?"

Amy shook her head. "I'm coughing more than I'd like, and I'm so tired. I just want to sleep for a week."

"You may end up doing just that. I'll do my best to get you back to full health soon. The doctor will be here Friday to check on you again."

"What's today?" Amy asked, confused.

"Wednesday. So two more days until we see the doctor."

Amy finished the broth and handed Caroline the bowl and spoon. "Thank you for taking care of me."

"It's my pleasure." Caroline leaned down and kissed Amy's forehead and walked toward the door. "Would you like some more water?"

"Yes, please."

Caroline smiled. Amy remembered her manners even when she was so sick. She got the girl's water and made some tea with honey like her mother had given her many times when she'd had a cough.

Taking the tea and water upstairs, she sat on the edge of the bed while Amy drank all of the tea. "That should really help the cough."

"Thank you." Amy drank it down and handed Caroline the cup. "I think I'm going to sleep again."

"Sounds good. And if you need me during the night, just call out, and I'm sure I'll hear you."

Amy smiled and nodded, quickly curling up so she could sleep more.

Chapter Ten

BY MONDAY, AMY WAS feeling better, and no one else had gotten the illness. Caroline was relieved to know Amy was going to be all right. On Amy's first trip down the stairs after being in bed for so long, Caroline and Victoria showed her the three dresses they'd made for her.

Amy stood with a huge smile on her face, reaching for the Sunday dress. "Caroline, you made me a collar like Victoria's!"

Caroline shook her head. "Victoria made it for you. Didn't she do a great job?"

"You helped," Victoria said, "but I did most of it."

"I love it. Thank you both for working so hard on it while I lay in bed reading." Amy took all three dresses. "I'm going to go upstairs and try them on."

"No, go into the bedroom down here. I don't want you running up and down the stairs with as sick as you were." Even though she was better, Caroline was still worried. She'd get over it eventually, she knew, but for now, she was going to be careful with her.

Amy nodded, hurrying away. She tried the dresses on, coming out wearing each one. "They fit perfectly. I love them."

Caroline exchanged a look with Victoria. The two of them had worked very hard to get them finished. "Now we need to make one more for Victoria, and then we can take a short sewing break before we start on your petticoats and nightgowns."

"How did you get them done so quickly?" Amy asked, shaking her head. "Victoria's dress took a long time."

Caroline led Amy over to the new sewing machine. "With this. You'll be using it soon, too."

"Wow. Dad gave you this? When?"

"He brought it the afternoon you got sick, so last Wednesday."

"What day is it now?" Amy asked, perplexed.

"Monday," Victoria told her. "You were sick a long time."

"We missed church?"

"I stayed home with you, and your Dad took Victoria. It gave me time to do more sewing." Caroline hadn't minded missing church too much. She liked to go every week, but Amy's health was a great deal more important.

"Thank you." Amy walked into the parlor, her book tucked under her arm. "I think I'm going to sit in here and read today, instead of staying in bed."

Caroline found her a quilt and covered her with it. "There. Now you'll be just fine. Do you want me to bring you some water? More tea with honey?"

Amy shook her head, even as she stifled a cough. "I really am better. Just let me sit here and read."

"We're about to do the laundry. Do you want us to take a chair outside, and you can sit in it and watch?"

Amy nodded eagerly. "I don't usually like to watch other people do chores, but I've been in my room for so long, I'm eager for company."

When Andrew walked into the house at the end of the day and saw Amy sitting in the parlor, he hurried to her. "You're better?"

She nodded. "I really am. Caroline hasn't let me do anything all day but sit here."

He laughed. "I think she made the right choice." Amy's voice was still a little hoarse from being so sick, but his worries for her were gone. If Caroline let her out of bed, then she really must be better.

After the girls were in bed that night, Caroline sat with him, crocheting another collar. She enjoyed doing them, and she knew the girls wanted to give them to friends as Christmas gifts that year. Andrew sat whittling one of his animals, and they worked together in contented silence.

"Thank you," Andrew said suddenly, breaking through the calm.

"For what?" Caroline genuinely had no idea what he was thanking her for. She had only done what she'd come there to do. She'd been a mother and a wife.

"For all you've done for Amy. For what you've done for Victoria. She's a totally different girl since you arrived. I had no idea she would ever learn to smile again."

"I keep waiting for her to get angry with me, but she just does as she's asked. I've been very pleased with both of them."

Andrew smiled. "I don't think you have any idea how much you've changed our entire world. When I sent for you, I never expected to fall in love. I truly just wanted a housekeeper who would make sure the girls stayed in line and who got things done. I mainly wanted a hot meal on the table when I got home every night."

She shrugged. "I'm glad you've gotten what you wanted out of the arrangement." She wasn't holding out for love anymore. He'd made it clear to her that he didn't want that from her at all. As much as she loved him, she could never tell him about her feelings.

"What I'm trying to say—and obviously not doing a very good job of—is that I love you with everything inside me. You came here, and you not only changed my girls and my home, but you changed my heart. I thought it would be frozen forever after losing my Marie, but instead, I want to spend the rest of my life with you."

She frowned at him for a moment, thinking about what he'd said. "You don't have to say that to me because you think I expect it. I know I came here with unrealistic expectations, and they've changed over the weeks. I know that you still love your first wife."

"I do still love her, and I always will. She provided me with two beautiful daughters, and she died trying to provide a son. But that doesn't mean I can't love you as well. It's like you told the girls when you first got here. You're not taking the place of their mother. You're just asking for a place in their hearts as well."

She smiled. "You really mean it? You love me?"

Andrew laughed. "Do I seem like the kind of man who would tell you I love you when I don't?"

She pursed her lips for a moment as if thinking about his question, but finally she shook her head. "No, you don't. Does this mean you're going to write love poems to me?" Caroline had to laugh at the girl she'd been when she'd taken the train to him. She'd honestly thought they would write love poems to each other and read them aloud in front of a fire. He was not the kind of man who would ever dream of doing something like that, and she wouldn't even want him to try to be someone he wasn't.

"I don't think so. I mean, if it's what you really need from me, I can try, but . . ."

She laughed, shaking her head. "No, that's not what I need from you at all. I just need to know that you love me. And I need you to know that I love you. I loved you before I ever saw you when I thought you were someone totally different. But now I know the real you, and I love you so much more."

"Really? You do?" He took her hand in his, gazing into her eyes. "Even though I'm not someone who feels the need to sing you love songs?"

She nodded. "I really do. I love you for who you are, and I love your girls. I love them so much. I hope you know that I wouldn't trade them for anything."

"I do know that." He leaned over and kissed her softly. "I think they need a brother."

"And more sisters. Maybe I can have nine girls and one boy . . . I think I'm a good girl mom."

"You are a good girl mom, but you'd make a good *boy* mom, too!"

Caroline sighed. "I'll just have as many babies as God gives me and love them all. How's that?"

"That sounds like a solution I can agree with."

Epilogue

TEN YEARS AND FOUR daughters later . . .

Caroline looked over at Victoria and Amy, who were there helping out with their younger sisters. It was almost time for her to give birth to her fifth child, and she was moving so much slower than usual. "I'm so glad you girls were willing to come over and help out."

Victoria was pregnant with her first, and Amy was newly married. They both were extremely devoted to her and had come to be her support. "We're always willing to help you, Mother," Amy told her. They'd decided to call her Mother instead of Mom, because they wanted to keep her in her own spot, not in the place of their beloved mom.

Victoria nodded, putting a hand on the side of her stomach. "He kicked!"

"He might be a she," Caroline said with a laugh. "Look how many shes we have running around here."

Her youngest had just turned two, and she ran to Caroline. "Mama!"

"Yes, Betty."

"When will you have the baby? I want a little sister!"

Caroline had long since given up on the idea of ever having a boy. Girls were all she had, and she was content with that. Andrew said he was content, but she could tell he still dreamed of her having a little boy. "Soon, sunshine."

Betty hurried off to play with her sisters, and Caroline sat down, her hand going to her stomach. "I think it's time for someone to go fetch the midwife. My contractions are getting close." Her water had broken hours before, and they all knew they were on baby watch.

Amy nodded. "I'll go tell Dad." She hurried out the door.

Andrew was working on the barn that day, knowing that he'd be off to fetch the midwife soon. He didn't mind staying close to home, especially when there was a new baby to be born. As he saddled his horse, he said a quick prayer that this one would *finally* be a boy. After six girls, he needed to have another man in the house. How was he going to possibly fight off all the suitors that were sure to come calling without help?

He loved his girls, every last one of them. He'd thought for sure he was going to have a boy when Caroline had gotten pregnant so soon after they married. But then Anne was born. Then came Sally. And Georgia. Finally, there was little Betty, who was a spitfire. He wasn't sure how many more pregnancies he could go through. The pickle cravings with the other four had been bad enough, but this pregnancy, Caroline had needed something absolutely repulsive. She'd wanted diced pickles on her apple pie. He gagged every time he thought about it, and he had to leave the room before she ate it.

He was back forty-five minutes later, and the midwife was following in her wagon. "I need a boy this time," he whispered to her as she hurried in.

The midwife waved him away as she went inside to do her job. She had delivered all of his children, and he could just wait and see what the baby was like every other father.

An hour later, a stunned midwife stepped into the parlor where Andrew was pacing, a baby in each arm. "You got your wish." She handed him first one son and then the other. "I'm going to finish seeing to your wife, but you can hold your sons."

"Sons. I never expected even one son, but twins? What are we ever going to name the two of you?" He was too busy looking between the two boys, his heart filling with joy, to notice when the midwife left the room. "I know. Jacob and Nicholas. We'll call you Nick and Jake. My sons."

Never an emotional man, he felt tears pricking his eyes. When he was finally allowed to see his wife, he walked into the room, and she had a grin that truly transformed her face. "Sons."

"Two sons. I can't believe we finally got boys."

She smiled, reaching her arms out for one of them. "What will we call them? I only thought of girls names, because I never thought we'd actually have a boy!"

"What would you think of Nicholas and Jacob?"

She nodded. "I think it's fitting that you name them whatever you want. You have your boys."

Andrew leaned down and kissed her softly. "Thank you for giving me sons. And daughters. I love you with everything inside me."

"I love you right back. Thanks for making all my dreams come true."